Not That Kind of Call Girl

by

Nova García

The Wild Rose Press, Inc.
PO Box 708
Adams Basin, NY 14410-0708
Visit us at www.thewildrosepress.com

Publishing History
First Edition, 2024
Trade Paperback ISBN 978-1-5092-5508-5
Digital ISBN 978-1-5092-5509-2

Published in the United States of America

Dedication

To R, my everything and then some.
Special thanks to The Wild Rose Press staff and Judi,
my editor, who patiently guided me in polishing my
manuscript from a rock into a gem.

Chapter One

November 9, 2016
The Cascade City Chronicle

"Otter Devastation, Harmful Chemicals Discovered in Pacific Northwest Otter Population"

Julia Navarro-Nilsson likened her supervisor job in *The Cascade City Chronicle* call center to juggling—not bowling pins, beanbags, or balls, but cranky customers, wacky employees, and a skirt-chasing boss.

Outside of work, she had:

weekly pregnancy checkups (Dr. Folger, Fridays, four p.m.)

a get-ready-for-baby checklist (ninety-two percent complete)

a birthing class with her husband, Charlie (one left—Saturday, ten a.m., Triton Hall, room two)

a self-help book club (current read: *Your Life, Your Way)*

everything else life throws at you when you're not looking

Her maternity leave would start in two weeks, and she'd get some much-deserved downtime to enjoy her new baby come hell or high amniotic water.

Except "downtime" and "new baby" were oxymorons.

Rookie mistake.

****

Julia sat in her gray-walled cubicle, tidying her desk. Everything had its place: sharpened pencils, lined yellow notepad, tape dispenser, cell phone charger, and coffee mug placed with the handle to the right. Her cell phone chimed at twelve fifty-five p.m. Planting her feet a shoulder's-width apart, she pushed herself to a stand, grabbed the interview packet, and filed past rows of Customer Service Representatives or "CSRs" taking calls.

"Cascade City Chronicle, this is Sistine. He threw it in a puddle? Heavens to Betsy, I'm super sorry about that. I'll get a new paper right out."

"Cascade City Chronicle, Gertie speaking. Uh-huh. Well, no, Mrs. Finkelstein—we don't approve of newspaper carriers kicking people's dogs."

Julia lumbered toward the front lobby to collect her job applicant.

****

Carmen Cooper, a petite young woman with skin the color of walnuts, silky black hair, and striking amber eyes, stood at *The Cascade City Chronicle* reception desk.

Julia extended a hand. "I'm Julia Navarro-Nilsson. Thanks for coming in."

Carmen's right arm stayed at her side. Paper towels and masking tape wrapped around two of her fingers. "The pleasure is all mine," she replied in a Spanish-accented voice. "Thank you for meeting with me."

Julia drew her eyebrows together and gestured toward Carmen's hand. "I hope that doesn't hurt too much. Do you want me to find a splint in one of our first-aid kits?"

"No, ma'am. It's kind of you to offer."

Julia led Carmen down a long sterile-looking hallway. "How about some water? It'll come in one of those high-class triangle paper cups."

Carmen shook her head.

Julia pointed to a small conference room with jaundiced 1970s lighting and stiff-backed metal chairs. "As you know from the job posting, we have a part-time customer service position in the call center, evenings and weekends. Why don't you tell me about yourself, your work history, and why you want the job. Then I'll tell you about the company, what the CSR position entails, and ask you a few questions. Sound good?"

"Yes, ma'am. I spend most of my time studying for school. As for work history, I've mostly done housekeeping. Well, I've *only* done housekeeping, but I am a quick learner and graduated near the top of my class." Carmen looked up shyly through enviably long lashes. "I need a job to pay for books and expenses. And of course, I love people."

They all say they 'love people' until the first subscriber calls them an idiot and tells them to shove the paper up their ass, Julia thought as she scanned Carmen's résumé. "I see your employer's name, Percy Booth, but you don't specify where or give a phone number." Julia tapped her pencil eraser on the table. "Percy Booth—Percy Booth—that name sounds familiar. Is he on the city council? Or the school board?"

Carmen's right leg bounced. The ruffles at the hemline of her baby blue shirt rippled like a wave on a windy day.

"I'm sorry, I don't remember Mr. Booth's address."

"It's all right. People forget stuff on their

applications all the time. You can look it up before you go. Are you from around here?"

"Yes, ma'am—born and raised."

Julia set her pencil down, perfectly perpendicular to her notepad. "I'm a south Texas transplant myself, but you couldn't drag me away from Washington State. My husband and I love it here. We're surrounded by water and mountains. We make a lot of very fine wine, and mildew is our state flower. What's not to love?" She chuckled at her mildew joke. Carmen smiled politely.

Twenty miles north of Seattle, Cascade City, Washington, a beach town used for cheesy LoveLine Channel cult-classic movies, *Ding Dong Dead at Barnacle Beach* and *A Little Lighthouse Christmas,* drew 400,000 tourists annually. Six thousand people, average age sixty-one, made it their year-round home.

The interview came to a close.

"Will you be calling Mr. Booth?" Carmen asked.

Julia nodded to the bulging baby belly blocking the view of her feet. "Yes, later today. I don't have much time to decide and get someone on board."

"His memory's not too good anymore."

"Does he know he's a reference? It's best to give advance notice."

Carmen picked at a hangnail. "We did not stay in touch." She leaned forward and pointed to the résumé. "I wrote the name of my high school English teacher, here, you see?"

"I'll try to call her, but your work reference is the most important one, and Percy Booth's the only one you've got."

****

The two women stood in the lobby. Carmen cupped

Julia's hand between hers the way you might hold a moth before setting it free.

"Thank you for interviewing me, and I hope to see you again. I want this job very, very much," Carmen said. "Please."

"*Mucho gusto, Carmen. Que le vaya bien*."

Carmen's eyes opened wide in surprise. "*Y usted también*." She turned and exited the leaded glass doors into the soggy autumn afternoon.

Tall, with raven-black hair and creamy white skin, people guessed Julia was Greek or Italian—never Latina, even other Latinos. She watched Carmen run to the bus stop across the street, using her hands to shield the drizzly rain. Julia pinched her lower lip. *She interviewed well, but she was anxious and fidgety. No big deal—everybody gets the interview jitters.*

****

Julia sat at her desk and opened her "Shit to Do Before Baby" spreadsheet:

Hire CSR

Write the budget

Approve/deny vacation requests

Schedule/plan holiday potluck

Call facilities dude to replace flickering light tubes and three broken chairs, plus clean the icky sticky blinds

Performance evaluations: Monty, Sistine, Walt

Get good-for-nothing Carlton to hire my leave of absence backfill

Train my backfill

"Might as well start at the top of the list," she muttered. First, she needed Percy Booth's address. In all the conversation, she'd forgotten to have Carmen fill it in.

findpeople.com showed:

Percy A. Booth

6688 Overlook Drive

Cascade City, WA

425-555-1935

She turned the application over.

Applicant Name: Carmen Cooper

Applicant Address: 6688 Overlook Drive, Cascade City, WA

They have the same address? What the hell?

Julia called Mr. Booth. It rang three times before someone picked up.

"Yes?" came a deep voice.

"Hello, this is Julia Navarro-Nilsson from *The Cascade City Chronicle*. May I speak with Percy Booth?"

She heard a click.

"Hello? Hello? I'm not trying to sell you something, you schmuck." She thrust her middle finger at the phone. "And you're not getting off that easy. I'll call you again at four p.m." She added it to the checklist.

Call schmuck Booth

Chapter Two

November 9, 2016 — continued

Bending over at the middle to riffle through a file cabinet felt like the aftermath of three rounds through the all-you-can-eat taco bar wearing jeans two sizes too small. *Seriously? My maternity underwear's too tight?*

"Jesus, Julia. Your ass is wide as an eighteen-wheeler," her boss, Carlton, said as he rounded the corner, making the clicking sound one might make when signaling a horse.

She straightened up slowly, folder in hand, tossed her dark ringlets over her shoulder, and pressed a hand against her low back.

"Oh yeah? I'm gestating a human. What's your excuse for that thing?" She raised her eyebrows and glanced at his beach ball belly.

"Awww—don't spoil it, sweetie. I was having a little fun. I kind of like your ass before and after you got knocked up. Now come into my office. We gotta talk."

Julia tightened her jaw. "I'm big as a beluga and seriously hormonal, so can you do me a favor and imitate a decent human being? I've told you before to stop that shit."

Carlton ignored her and walked through the call center. She waddled behind. The reader board on the wall blinked:

On Hold: 20

Average Wait Time: 3:14

The night before, bajillionaire businessman Sterling Wolfe had won the presidency. *The Cascade City Chronicle* could count on increased call volumes whenever a big news story broke, like when:

Navy SEALs killed Osama Bin Laden

Michael Jackson died

Prince Charles and Lady Diana Spencer married

Prince Charles and Lady Diana Spencer divorced

the CDC confirmed the first US case of Ebola

the newspaper came with half-off coupons for compression socks, pill organizers, arthritis cream, and earwax removal kits, popular with the sixty-plus crowd

Julia paused just outside Carlton's office door. "Is everyone here and on the phones?" she asked Kelvin, the call center lead.

"I'm checkin' the schedule right now," he answered.

"All right. This shouldn't take long, but send a search party if I don't come out within five minutes." She stepped into Carlton's office strewn with newspapers, crushed triangle paper cups, candy wrappers, a tobacco tin, and a "Golfers Make Better Swingers" mug half-filled with phlegm.

"Here's the problem," Carlton said. "Who's gonna do your job when *that* thing shows up?"

Julia studied the office chair and remained standing. She didn't want the backside of her pink maternity dress, a design mashup of tent meets Pepto Bismol, to touch the indeterminate gray stain on the seat cushion.

"Come on, Carlton. I'm your only direct report, and it's your job to figure out coverage."

He waved his hand around. "I can't be bothered with administrative tasks like—staffing. I've been busy with other things—*muy im-por-tawn-tay* things, at the direction of the publisher, I might add."

Right. Since when do you interact with the publisher? "I recommended Kelvin as my backfill over a month ago. The temporary assignment form's in the folder." She set it on his desk. "Fill it out and give it to Human Resources. Or do it online. There's a forms section on the manager intranet."

"*You* fill it out, and I'll sign it later." Carlton pushed the folder at her. "I'm leaving for an off-site meeting. They'll have donuts there. The ones with butterscotch."

"What's it about?"

"Pfft. I can't tell *you*. It's a secret, baby doll, but it's a big fucking deal, and you'll hear about it soon enough. Now do something about all those calls on hold. What do these people want from us?"

"I dunno—the newspaper? You really are a dim bulb."

"What a buncha whiners." He pulled out a cigarette, stuck it between his lips, and left.

Julia stepped out, grabbed a chair, and plopped down next to Kelvin, a champion wrestler and weightlifter from Oklahoma City Christian College with the muscles to match.

"You gonna hire the person you interviewed this mornin'?" he asked. "We runnin' awfully thin."

"I don't know. Something's fishy about her." *Like, she's a liar.* "But I kinda like a mystery. I'm sure I'll figure it out."

"I hope you do 'cause," he said, folding his lips inward as if preventing something from escaping, "you

9

don't got much time left. I mean, it looks like you swallowed one of them little round cars from the 1960s."

"That's exactly how it feels. The little guy's pushed my stomach into my throat, and my bladder's his trampoline. Look at my feet." She held out her legs. "Classy shoes, eh?" She pointed to her flip-flops and feet resembling puffy yeast bread rising and ready for the oven. "It was either these or my penguin slippers. Nothing else fits."

"My momma's feet look like that, and she's not even pregnant." He smiled. "But don't tell her I said that. How long ya plannin' to be on leave?"

"Three months. And you'll be the temporary supervisor. Congratulations, Kelvin."

He flashed his high-wattage smile, his ultra-white teeth appearing all the whiter, surrounded by his complexion, a rich shade of espresso with a splash of milk. "I feel like I'm floatin'."

"Don't float too far, my friend. We've got nine customers on hold."

"Gertie called. She's havin' trouble gettin' her kids off to school, but that was two hours ago. She shoulda been in by now."

"Would you call her, please? If it's her car again, I can pick her up."

"You're like the house mom at my frat, always worryin' about everybody, helpin' 'em when they're in trouble, bakin' 'em cookies. What kinda boss does that?"

"You're nice, too."

"Ya gave everyone a mug with cocoa and mini marshmallows last week. All *sixteen* of us."

"And your point?" Julia reached for some loose papers, straightened them into a neat pile, and, unsatisfied, straightened them again.

"Ya sent my momma a get-well card, and ya don't even know 'er."

"I bet your momma loved it."

"I cannot tell a lie; she surely did."

****

Julia didn't see Gertie or any other employee again for months; call schmuck Booth, finish the budget, give the evaluations, or anything else on her list. Her water broke before she made it to her desk.

Six squares of industrial carpet did not survive the incident.

"Damn," she mumbled on her way out. "You're two weeks too early, *chiquito*, and I don't much care for surprises."

Chapter Three

November 9, 2016 — afternoon

Carmen left her Introduction to Greek Philosophy class and hurried to her English class: Writing and Self-Awareness. The bitter wind whooshing between buildings pierced the jean jacket she got in sixth grade from the Clothes for Kids charity bus. Her toes felt stiff with cold inside her thin black tennis shoes.

She entered the auditorium. Every guy who wasn't staring at his phone turned to watch her go up the steps. She pretended not to notice. Taking her seat, she wrapped her arms tightly around her middle and rubbed her hands up and down the tops of her arms.

The projection screen illuminated the room with its bright white background and black letters.

"An award-winning author once wrote that she no longer wanted reminders of time lost to wasted efforts and her past broken life. Do you identify with this philosophy? Why or why not? Write a minimum two-hundred-word response, double-spaced. Submit by close of business, November eighteenth."

Carmen let the words sink in. Her mind began to race, and her pulse picked up speed.

She had *some* good life experiences: helping Mami in the kitchen, playing *Lotería* with the brightly colored cards and pinto beans for game pieces, singing quietly in Mami's bedroom, oh so quietly—her the melody and Mami the harmony, her and Mami brushing and braiding each other's hair before bed—the sound of Mami's voice.

But in that house, the God-awful outweighed the good. 2017, she decided, would be the year of salvation. And, if she could get up the nerve, retribution.

Her stomach clenched, and a foul taste rose in her mouth. She ran down the auditorium steps and made it to the bathroom just in time to throw up.

****

The sun fell below the horizon at four forty-five p.m., early but not unexpected in a Northwest November. Carmen sat against a wall in her furniture-free bedroom and opened her spiral-bound notebook from English class. She unwrapped the paper towels and tape, wiggled her bruised fingers, and recalled when they got twisted until she fell to the floor—all because the grilled cheese she served had cheddar, not the preferred Swiss.

"Assignment due November eighteenth. An award-winning author once wrote that she no longer wanted reminders of time lost to wasted efforts and her past broken life. Do you identify with this philosophy? Why or why not?"

Carmen shifted from sitting cross-legged to laying flat on her back, then onto her stomach and back to cross-legged as she stewed about the assignment.

I'm afraid I must disagree with the author she wrote in loose, loopy letters since it hurt to bend her fingers. *She wasn't talking about an inanimate object like a candy cane or coffee cup; she was talking about someone's life. And what got lost wasn't a set of keys or*

13

*a sock; it was a person. Ignoring a painful past can only
lead to more of the same.*

Carmen took a cleansing breath, padded over to her
closet, and pulled out a wide shoe box labeled "They Call
Me Blaze, 1965, Spectacle Studios" that once held a pair
of men's size thirteen cowboy boots. Inside the box, she
kept a stash of books—an encyclopedia, dictionary,
thesaurus, and three of her favorite Shakespeare plays—
Hamlet, *Othello*, and *Romeo and Juliet*. And an old
diary. "Time for some inspiration," she whispered as she
lifted the diary, arranged her thick mane into a messy
bun, and secured it with the hairband around her wrist.
She opened it to her first entry, age ten, Christmas day.

Fifth Grade

December 25, 2008

Dear Monica,

*I got you as a present from Mrs Alfonso in the libary
at scool. I lik her. She shares her sandwich sometimes
when I dont have a lunch. She said every girl should have
a dairy. A place where she can rite her thots. Now that I
am ten and practicly a teen ager I have lots of things to
tell u. I have a crush on Jake Dixon and I think he likes
me to! Im calling u Monica becuz its my favrit name and
its better then calling u dairy. One day if I have a baby
girl I will name her Monica after u. Or maybe Ashlie. Or
Lillie. Or Tiffanie. The IE makes the names sooooo much
more intresting dont you think? Mami was sad again this
morning. Shes like that alot but it gets bad at Christmas.
It makes me sad to. She cries when she talks about
Christmas in Mexico. Why cant she be happy with me
and Papa Percy? She told me the Mexico stories a
million times. Its warm there during Christmas. Not like
here. Families decorat there houses with flowers and*

green branchs and leaves. They cut shapes in little brown paper bags and put a candle in each one and set them on side walks, window sells, and roofs to make the nieghborhood pretty. They have a posada starting December sixteen. I wont even tell you about it cuz its a big deal and has lots of parts to it and my hand is getting tired. I wish I could go to Mexico sometime especially at Christmas. That way Mami would be happy on Christmas morning. Weve never even been outside Cascade City and Mexico is very far away. Papa Percy sez we can never go cuz mami will probly get killed there.

Ur best friend,

Carmen Cooper

PS Mami sez thats not my real last name but I cant tell anybody not even u so papa Percy and Mami can never read this. Shhh. A girls dairy is seecret.

Chapter Four

November 10, 2016
The Cascade City Chronicle

"Cascade City Senior Swingers Host an Evening of Square Dance Fun"

Julia's pregnancy-plumped butt sat atop a cold metal bedpan. Truthfully, the bedpan disappeared under there. Jazz played softly in the background. Monitors whirred and blinked, and the second hand on the wall clock ticked. Charlie looked at her, his blue-green eyes as big as bottlecaps. The pretty, young nurse with the bouncy blonde ponytail raised her eyebrows, sucked in her plump lower lip, and held her breath.

Never was there a more anticipated BM.

"Nope, ain't happenin'," Julia announced.

Nurse Cheerful patted Julia's arm to comfort her because she failed her basic instruction to poop in a pot.

Julia's eyes flew open, and she gritted her teeth. "Oh. Dear. God. Here comes another one."

The contractions came every two minutes. As the pain climbed to the pinnacle of the labor roller coaster, her patience plummeted down the other side.

"Breathe, Missus Navarro-Nilsson, breathe," Nurse Perky said.

Julia's face flushed red, and she released a

hurricane-force breath. "Look, I'm pretty sure there's a bowling ball in my ass, so excuse me if I'm not doing this right."

"A bowling ball? Oh. I know what's happening." The nurse looked up as if an actual lightbulb had turned on. "It's not a bowel movement; it's the baby. Every time you have a contraction, it pushes the baby downward, putting pressure on your rectum."

"There's a baby in my rectum?" Julia wiped sweaty curls from her face and white pasty goobers from the corners of her mouth.

"Oh no, Missus Navarro-Nilsson. It's back labor. Most babies come out with their faces down, but yours is sunny side up. That's what's causing your low back pain."

"What can I do for you, honey?" Charlie wrung his hands. "I want to help."

Pain ripped through Julia's low back. "Turn off the goddamn music!" Poor, sweet Charlie—she couldn't remember the last time she'd raised her voice at him. Then again, yelling might be a reasonable reaction to passing a human through a hole the diameter of a soda can.

"The instructor in birthing class told us to make a playlist as part of her labor plan. Julia picked all the jazz greats," Charlie said. "She made a list with the songs in a particular order—she's very organized like that. I brought it with me if you want to see it. It's in the bag on the chair."

"Do you like rap?" the nurse asked.

"For the love of God, Charlie. Turn. It. Offffff," Julia screeched.

"I can see you're upset, Missus Navarro-Nilsson,"

Nurse Obvious said. "It's perfectly normal, and it *has* been, oh"—she glanced at her glitter light purple smartwatch—"nearly twelve hours since you started. Let's see how far you've progressed, shall we?" She walked around to the foot of the bed, put her porcelain-skinned face between Julia's purplish, splotchy, stirrupped legs, and peered up and over her crotch. "I better get Dr. Folger."

****

Nine-pound, twenty-one-and-a-half-inch Charles Arthur Nilsson the Third arrived at ten p.m.

Since they didn't need another Charlie or Charles in the family, and this baby was Charles Nilsson the Third, and three is *tres* in Spanish, they called him Trey. Trey Nilsson, a nod to Julia's Mexican heritage and Charlie's Swedish maternal side. "Swexican," as Julia liked to say. Or "Mexidish." Full head of dark-brown hair, long fingers, chubby cheeks, and giant grayish-sure-to-turn-brown eyes. The very essence of baby perfection. A miracle.

How could an egg the thickness of a strand of hair and a sperm twenty-five thousand times smaller than a ping-pong ball meet on a chance occasion and make a squishy little stranger with a disturbingly pointy head?

****

December 2, 2016
The Cascade City Chronicle
"Pacific Crest Energy Raises Rates"

Three weeks passed, and motherhood felt as natural as—as natural as—well, it didn't feel natural. It felt strained. It felt—wrong. Julia and motherhood paired as well as chilled champagne and chili fries. It didn't help that she had Trey at the bleakest time of year—dark before dinner, drizzly most of the time, and with a heating bill that she and Charlie couldn't afford to pay if they turned the temperature up past sixty-four degrees. If only Creepy Carlton would retire so she could get his job and the pay increase that came with it.

In the months before she hurried out of the employee exit, amniotic fluid running down her legs, she couldn't wait to get out of there. But post-Trey, late at night, when every nerve stood at attention as she waited for Trey to wake up, she wondered how Kelvin was doing in the management role. What meeting was Carlton going to—something about *a big-fucking-deal* and *at the direction of the publisher*? Did he finish the budget? The call center was heading into the year's busiest season, and she never hired a CSR. Egad. She didn't solve the mystery of Carmen Cooper's home address matching Percy What's-His-Name's. And was anybody monitoring the supply room and keeping it tidy? Was dust piling up on her desk and ergonomic keyboard? Twenty to fifty percent of dust comes from dead skin cells. Barf. Did someone replace the carpet squares her uterus defiled?

Maternity leave passed at the speed of—a slug on Valium. Every excruciating hour, she went through the motions. Feed the baby. Change the poopy baby. Hold the constantly cranky baby. Burp the squirmy annoying fussy baby. Pace the floor holding the damn why-did-I-have-this crybaby? baby. "It must be hard being a tiny person in a big world," she mumbled as she made the loop around their eight-hundred-square-foot house: family room, kitchen, baby room, family room, kitchen, baby room. "It must be hard being a tiny person in a big world. It must be hard being a tiny person in a big world." Hunched over and her shoulders burning, her tears fell and soaked through the thin cotton blanket she swaddled him in.

By midafternoon, she sat sideways on one butt cheek with a folded comforter under her backside, where her nether region had ripped from here to eternity. Trey curled around her middle, asleep on her lap. She studied his features.

Charlie's measly Swedish chromosomes never stood a chance in the heredity boxing ring.

Swedish Genes: Would you mind if I snuck in here and gave the child light-colored eyes? I mean, I hate to impose or offend, but blue eyes would be lovely, don't you think?

Latino Genes: Look, you monochromatic gringo-boy. Don't choo mess wit me. Mexicano genomes ees muy macho. We eat your kine for breakfast. Ees brown all the way, man. Brown hair, brown eyes, brown everyting. Now, get outta here 'fore I whoop your scrawny DNA.

"Can we take him back?" Julia murmured, her chin wobbling.

"Take him back?" Charlie frowned, mug in hand. "What do you mean?"

"We could float him on a river in a reed basket, so an Egyptian queen could find him and raise him as Pharaoh. It worked for Moses. This baby cries; no, he *screams* all the effin' time, Charlie. His naps last twenty minutes. He's latched onto me six hours a day; I added it up. This baby is sucking the life out of me six hours a day. You know how I've felt like a cow all my life? Now, I'm *actually* a cow. Someone is milking me, Charlie. I haven't done laundry in a week; the sheets feel like they're going to get up and walk off the bed by themselves, and something in the fridge smells like rotting fish meets Pleistocene-era cheese. And the clutter? I'm losing my mind here. Oh, and the dust. There are skin cells in there." She wrinkled her nose. "Skin cells. Eeewww."

The corners of Charlie's mouth twitched. "We're learning as we go—nothing wrong with that. It's going to get easier. The teachers at school say so," he added as if it helped. "Do you want me to take him? Or get you some orange juice? Maybe a little sugar would do you good."

I ate half a bag of Halloween candy while you slept last night, and it didn't help. "No, thanks. I'm okay." *I am not okay.*

"Whatever you need, babe." His voice sounded as buoyant as a pin-pricked balloon. A cloud loomed over Charlie's usually sunny disposition. He managed thirty-one noisy, needy first-graders at school from eight a.m. to three p.m. and comforted a depressed, exhausted bellyacher at home.

And he took care of Trey, too.

Julia ran her fingers through her unwashed curls. "I'll keep him with me for now." She wiped her snotty nose and lip with a used tissue from a pile of more used tissues. "I love you. You've been so patient with me." She wagged her finger. "Come hither, my love."

The poor guy—her gorgeous, sweet hunk of Scandinavian exquisiteness deserved some affection, even if she didn't feel affectionate. Or attractive. Or clean-haired.

Charlie moved in; she wrapped her hand behind his head and pulled him toward her. His tongue hungrily probed her mouth; she tugged his lower lip and sucked on it as if she were massaging the juice out of a plump summer strawberry.

"I've missed you," Charlie said, gazing down her T-shirt at her bare breasts. His light eyes sparkled with a coating of tears as he reached in and brushed his fingers over her left nipple—which leaked—then sprayed milk—like a hose with a thumb over the nozzle.

Julia grabbed a burp cloth, shoved it under her shirt to cover one breast, and tried to attach Trey to the other. "Well, that didn't turn out too well."

"It's not your fault, babe. It's getting hard to resist you, though."

Julia nodded toward the bulge in his sweatpants. "I see that."

The sparkle in Charlie's eyes faded. "I'll be grading papers in the kitchen if you need me, and I'll dust the house when I finish with them. Let me know if you want that orange juice."

Julia looked at the sleepy baby in her arms and kissed his chubby fist. "I love you, Trey," she said weakly, trying to mean it.

The new-mother thing was not at all like what *Baby's First Year* magazine depicted or what she'd read on the internet. Wasn't she supposed to love, love, love his velvety skin and soft feathery hair? His little squeaks and coos? Wasn't she supposed to feel an overwhelming sense of devotion and thank God every waking moment for their unbreakable mother-son bond?

Not so much.

She wanted to stick him in the hole from which he came.

This baby scared her shitless, with his neck all weak

and wonky and his nearly crossed, unfocused eyes. And she'd completed every action on her pregnancy checklist to prepare for the little booger.

She:

took the prenatal vitamins with the right combination of ingredients (made her constipated)

ate an unnatural amount of green leafy vegetables (kale. ugh)

kept her coffee intake to two cups (torture)

managed stress with Mommy-to-Be Yoga class (with a surprisingly strong contingent of women with hairy armpits)

joined a "nesting mothers" support group (too many worrywarts, malcontents, and positively positive people—gag me with a spoon)

rubbed coconut oil on her belly to prevent stretch marks (false advertising)

read *The Magical Miracle of Motherhood* four times from front to back (shithead author didn't warn her that she'd feel like an empty shell of her old self)

watched too many informational videos to count (homemade baby food! breastfeeding 101, baby rash treatments, baby massage, infant cradle cap remedies, why does your baby's belly button smell funky?), etc., etc.

A do-over—she wanted a do-over. And who talks about these things with other people—especially other mothers? Hell to the no. Mothers who loved their babies without trying made her want to spew.

So, she talked to Trey, a blob. "I'm sorry that I'm no good at this. It's not you; it's *me*."

Trey's eyes fluttered and opened. He scrunched his face, stiffened his torso, and wailed as if she was poking him with a shish kebab skewer.

"Maybe it *is* you." She hoisted herself to a stand, put him over her shoulder, patted his back, and repeated something that generations of Mexican mothers uttered before her: "*Sana, sana, colita de rana. Si no sanas hoy, sanarás mañana.* It means heal, heal, butt of a frog. If you don't heal today, you'll heal tomorrow." She shifted her feet from side to side, bouncing gently. "I'll have to teach you Spanish, *chiquito.*"

Trey grunted, farted, and settled down.

"It works, huh, *chiquito*? No one's ever been able to tell me what the butt of a frog has to do with it."

Chapter Five

December 16, 2016
The Cascade City Chronicle

"Local Teamsters Hold Fundraiser to Save Stumpy's Steakhouse"

Julia lay on the bed, damp from her shower, letting the ceiling fan dry her off. She eyed the curvy landscape below her neck. In addition to wider hips and a jiggly-as-a-jellyfish tummy, her once enviable breasts looked like undercooked pancakes sliding down a hill. The spikey hair on her usually velvety smooth armpits, legs, and crotch would draw blood if someone impaled themselves on it. Her cell phone rang when she reached for the bedspread to cover the unsightly mess.

"Hello?"

"Julia? It's Kelvin De la Fosse. Is this an okay time to talk?"

"Kelvin, you dork—I know what your last name is. What's up?" She padded over to Trey's room and peeked in. "And how many other 'Kelvins' do you think I know?"

"Sorry to bother ya. I hope you and the baby's doin' good."

"He's in his crib making spit bubbles. He's gifted, I tell you."

"I was just wonderin' if ya still wanna hire the young lady ya interviewed before ya left? Carmen Somethin'? She's called a few times. Says she got a job offer from a hamburger joint and turned it down. She's holdin' out for a job here. Our pay's pretty good for part-time, and she's right about that. We're comin' up on Christmas, Julia, and it's gettin' super busy. I'm hopin' ya wanna move ahead with Carmen?"

"Her last name's Cooper. I never did talk with her past employer—what was his name? Anyway, she's the only person I had in the hopper before I left. Ask Carlton to extend an offer."

"Any idea when you're comin' back? I like the temp job, but it's not the same with you not around."

"I don't know. I'll keep you posted. *Adios*, Kelvin De la Fosse. Thanks for running the place in my absence."

"Okay, nice talkin' to ya," he replied. "Have a great day."

Julia pressed the red circle on her phone. She was in no mood for someone in a good mood.

She pursed her lips and tapped them with an index finger. Percy Booth! That was the guy's name. He was Hollywood royalty from the 1960s, right up there with Steve McQueen, Gregory Peck, and Marlon Brando. Julia's father watched *Two-Kettle Sue*, *Gunslinger at Goldminers' Gorge,* and *A Man Called Spike* so many times she could still remember one of Booth's famous lines. "Yer gonna pay for whatcha done to Miss Lila, you boot-lickin' bastard."

"I knew there was something up with her. This could get interesting," she said to no one.

****

December 18, 2016
The Cascade City Chronicle
"City Council Strengthens Pooper Scooper Laws"

A call came in—the Mexican Hat Dance ring Julia programmed for her mother, Paloma.

"I'm gonna regret this," she said before answering the phone. "*Hola, Mamá.*"

"*Mija?* Why haven't you called me? How's my grandson?"

"I don't know, Mamá. Why haven't you called *me*? I'm the one who just had a baby."

"I was on a cruise around the British Virgin Islands. No cell service and I hate those newfangled phones anyway. The food was fabulous; the gift shop onboard was—let's just say—lacking. I *did* send you a card."

Julia was never one for deep conversations with her mother, a one-time small-town girl turned wealthy Dallas socialite, 5-Star hotel occupier, and bouffant hairdo enthusiast. But she needed to unload and found herself describing the birth in detail, the crying—both hers and Trey's—the sleepless nights, her emotional spikes, and the overwhelming fear that she stunk at motherhood.

"Julia, that poor child cries because you're so depressed," her mother said. "Babies can sense these things, and he must be very intuitive, like our side of the family. Mexicans are warm, feeling people. The Scandinavians tend to be on the colder, more detached side. Frigid, if you ask me."

"Mamá, I'm depressed because he always cries, not the other way around. I get almost no sleep. You try it for a while and see if you don't feel miserable."

"You slept through the night the day we brought you

27

home from the hospital. But—I have a way with babies—Mexican women always do." Paloma coughed.

"*I'm* Mexican, remember?"

"But you've been up *there* in—in—all that *greenery* for too long—living in a place only the Unabomber could love. Maybe my grandson's gassy. Have you tried giving him chamomile tea? Or a cinnamon stick steeped in hot water with honey? You *must* buy Mexican cinnamon. The kind you buy at MerryMart doesn't count."

"There aren't any MerryMart stores around here, and I don't know why he cries so much. Maybe he's got a headache or a fuzzy in his eye, he's too cold or too hot, he's bored, he's got a hair wrapped around his toes cutting off his circulation, or he wishes he had a different mother. Oh, bloody hell—hold on a sec." She pulled her ear away from the phone. "Shit. He's crying again, and I *just* put him down for a nap."

"Stop with the locker-room language, Julia. So uncouth. Are you eating too many raw onions? My grandson can probably taste that. Blech. Breastfeeding. How absolutely primeval. I gave you bottles—so much more civilized. You're probably eating pickled raw fish, like an Eskimo or a—Norwegian."

"Charlie's Swedish."

"There's a difference?"

"Mamá, this is not helping."

"Poor little Raúl. I can hear him. He sounds like a lost lamb. I guess I should have canceled my British Virgin Islands cruise. You're a mess."

"I *am* a mess. I'm a loser—a real dolt. Wait. Raúl?"

"Oh, come on, Julia. Trey's a foo-foo name if you ask me. They'll beat him to a pulp on the playground with a name like that."

"*Aye*, Mamá. I didn't ask you."

"Gotta run. I'm off to play cards—canasta this time. Graciela's hosting. That woman brought home a bulldog—against my strongest advice, I might add. Imagine the drool."

"Goodbye, Mamá."

"When can I visit? I'm not getting any younger, you know. We have things we need to discuss."

****

Carlton called not long after. "When are you coming to work? I miss the yummy smell of that coconut lotion you wear, and two CSRs just gave their notice, although I just hired some gal Kelvin mentioned. Gertie came in late twice last week, and someone saw Monty smoking a doobie in his car five minutes ago. What am I supposed to do with that?"

"Trey's not even two months old," Julia said.

"Oh. Yeah. How is the little ankle-biter?"

Ankle-biter? "I'm nowhere near ready to come back." *I want to come back!* "HR handles personnel issues."

"Don't you know HR stands for Hostile Repression? Or Highly Nasty?"

"That would be HN."

"Who gives a shit? Get your sweet ass in here. I need you. I'll be waiting here for you with bated breath."

"Bite me."

"What time?" Carlton laughed.

****

Carlton called three more times before Christmas, pleading with her to return, and each time, she declined. But, she reasoned, she could never find her old self if she stayed home.

Home, a former place of refuge and rejuvenation, had become a house of sadness and setbacks.

****

Julia ignored Thanksgiving. Charlie made a roast chicken with a side of canned pears. She frowned at the mere mention of Christmas—no decorations (pain in the ass), lighted tree (pain in the ass), or the traditional sexy Christmas Eve lingerie (no way would she flaunt her post-baby portly ass). Christmas morning, Charlie gave Julia a smooth rounded mother and child statue that he hand-carved from Balinese sugar wood. She had sex with him and pretended to like it.

She used to love sex. They'd go at it like rabbits—in bed, in the shower, on the kitchen table, against the washing machine, and in the woods, a thousand feet from the Mount Rainier Visitors' Center. In hindsight, the mountain sex might have gotten her into the predicament she found herself in.

"I miss you," Charlie said after lovemaking.

Julia frowned. "What do you mean?"

"The fireball I married." He released a long, slow breath. "I love you to the ends of the earth, no matter what, but I miss the fireball." He rolled over and turned out the light.

Chapter Six

January 7, 2017
The Cascade City Chronicle

"Cascade Cattle Farm Donates Dung to Community P-Patch Near School—Students In a Stink About the Stench"

Charlie got up with Trey at five a.m., gave him a bottle, and rocked him to sleep at seven thirty. Letting Charlie give him one bottle a day allowed Julia to sleep in now and then and make an occasional grocery store run by herself. Every minute she had without a kid crying or attached to a nipple helped. She felt sort of guilty about giving him a bottle. A *truly* devoted mother would nurse her *chiquito* one hundred percent of the time. *Baby Love Magazine* said Trey was too young for a bottle as it might disrupt the mother-child bond. *Screw Baby Love Magazine*, she told herself. *A bond? What bond?*

She pulled on a pair of gray sweats and wrapped herself in a squishy, comfy robe. A light rain drizzled, and the outside thermometer registered thirty-eight degrees. Condensation dripped down the single-paned windows of their ninety-one-year-old house, adding to the indoor chill. While Charlie lit a fire in the wood-burning stove, Julia brought in two bowls of Apple Cinnamon Os, two spoons, and napkins on bamboo trays. Charlie settled on the sofa. Julia straightened out the cream chenille throw blanket on the rocking chair so it hung at precisely the angle she saw in home decorating magazines and the Dori and Jon Love Where You Live! Show.

"Carlton wants me back," she said between spoonfuls.

Charlie set his bowl on the coffee table. "You mean he wants you to work so he can sleep at his desk."

"He's in all-day meetings with upper management. Something big's going on over there. He said so himself. I'll call Jerry later today. He'll know the scoop."

"Have you answered any of Jerry's texts or calls?" Charlie asked.

"No, and I'm sure he's royally pissed off with me. I haven't been in the mood for talking with friends—or humankind. Maybe we should get a dog, so I have a nonhuman to talk to."

"No," Charlie mouthed.

Jerry, her best bud and company busybody, covered arts and entertainment for *The Chronicle*. He wanted to be an investigative reporter, but there wasn't much to investigate; plus, the paper wasn't big enough to have a dedicated position. Aside from the occasional car prowl and porch pirate incident, the most scandalous story in Cascade City happened when a retired Florida senator got into a protracted battle with the city over a building permit. Whoop-dee-doo. But it didn't keep Jerry from looking for his big break to slink around, build alliances with underground sources, ask hard questions, and blow the lid off a juicy story of injustice, corporate greed, government misconduct, prostitution, etc.

Charlie threw up his hands and did his best "I'm

outraged" look, which came off as menacing as a gerbil. "I knew Carlton wouldn't leave you in peace. What a jerk. Seriously, I hate that guy." He tipped the cereal bowl and drank the milk. "Well, I guess 'hate' is a strong word. But I don't like him."

It took a lot to get on Charlie's bad side, and Julia had only told him about a fraction of Carlton's sexual innuendos and bigoted jokes. Carlton had no shame, tact, or lack of protruding nose hair, although he could act like a dignified business leader if it benefited him.

She'd thought about turning him in—many times— but wanted his job, and filing a complaint might backfire on her. Plus, the whole thing embarrassed her. Did she want to repeat lines like, "Do you have a sunburn, or are you always this hot?" to someone in a position of authority?

"Yes, Carlton's a turd, but this isn't about him. They've got a staffing shortage, Kelvin doesn't have the authority to hire people, and Carlton's MIA most of the time."

"What happens if you *don't* go back now?"

"I'm concerned about my employees, honey."

"Geez, Julia, go ahead. I can tell you've made up your mind anyway. I support you, hon. Whatever makes you happy, but I can't stand that boss of yours. No one should treat you with disrespect like that, and you shouldn't put up with it. That guy needs to be knocked down a notch—or ten."

"I'll call Kids' Korner and see if Trey can start on the sixteenth." Julia held a spoonful of cereal to her mouth and paused. "Oh crap. What am I going to wear?" She set the spoon down. "I still look six months pregnant."

Charlie held up his hands. "I don't know, babe."

"It was a rhetorical question, Charlie. You can eat anything you damn want and never gain weight. It's so unfair."

"You're beautiful just the way you are, Julia. Gorgeous even. A stunner."

"Uh-huh. I want to be someone who has to stand on a chair to reach the top shelf," she whined. "I want my feet to dangle when I sit on a barstool. I want to see my hip bones to prove they exist. Is that too much to ask?"

"Your dad was a big guy with a size-thirteen shoe. At least you come by it honestly."

At five feet eight inches tall, with size-nine feet, "big-boned," and big-boobed, she towered over every other female relative and family friend in her Mexican-American family.

"¡*Aye, tu hija es grandota*!" her mother's diminutive Mexican lady friends clucked during a card game the week of Julia's eighth birthday. To which her five-foot-nothing, ninety-pound mother, with wrists the diameter of churros, responded, "I just put her on the cabbage soup diet. You know I've tried *everything* else."

When the ladies left the house, a wounded and embarrassed Julia and Paloma loaded her light-colored and large-patterned clothing into a box for donation to the church.

"Light clothes make you look chunkier, *Mijita*," Paloma said. "Dark colors give the illusion of a longer and leaner frame. You can't go to school in *these*." She held up light blue corduroy pants in one hand and a cream-colored cotton shirt with a shiny panda design in the other. "Pull anything with horizontal stripes and large patterns out of your closet and drawers and put them in a garbage bag for the poor."

"*We're* poor, Mamá," Julia whispered.

"We get by. I'm trying to teach you something important here. Full skirts, puffy coats, skinny jeans, and wide belts must go. Belts cut your look in half, and we're aiming for svelte. No belts. No stripes. Do you understand?"

In fifth grade, the boys called her "Jumbo Julia." The one nice girl made pouty lips. "Don't you mind those nasty boys, Julia. You're fat, but you've got a pretty face."

By high school, she blossomed into an intelligent, hard-working, dark-eyed beauty with achievements that would impress any college admissions officer: GPA: four-point-zero, senior class president, drill team captain, state debate team champion, SAT score: fourteen sixty-six, and the Most Likely to Win a "Sophia Vergara Lookalike but Taller and with Curlier Hair Award," bestowed on her by fellow students.

Still, she avoided clothing on her mother's no-no list. What good would an impressive list of notable accomplishments be if all people thought was, "Too bad she's so fat."

Her scholarship to Seattle University brought her to Washington—the perfect coastal spot for a girl itching to leave the hella-hot Lonestar State with its giant cockroaches, cowboy hats, boots that made for sweaty feet, and a delicate-boned mother.

She graduated summa cum laude with a Bachelor's Degree in Business Administration, a Minor in Vocal Performance, and a ring on her finger from a hot Swede.

Standing proudly after her graduation ceremony, with honors cords and medals around her neck and

Charlie at her side, Paloma leaned in and spoke into her ear.

"Come to Texas and find one of your *own* kind to marry. This one's pale as a raw potato. And that sash around your neck is a horrid shade of green. It *doesn't* suit your skin tone."

****

January 15, 2017
The Cascade City Chronicle
"Lost Boa Constrictor May Be Linked to Poodle Disappearance"

Carmen sat in the school library and watched the people who came and went, inventing enviable life stories for each to escape her own. One student exited the elevator, pulled off her pink, lavender, and yellow ombre beanie cap, and shook her long blonde hair. A young man standing at a copy machine waved her over. They kissed to the woosh-woosh sound of papers sliding into a tray.

They'll get married, work at a tech company on the east side, live in a condo with a view of Lake Washington, and have two children in a program for the academically gifted. Her millionaire parents will invite them over for every holiday, and his flashy parents, who live nearby, will take them on cruises every summer.

She turned away from the couple, stared at her English assignment, and wondered what the professor would think of her response to the question about the author's quote and her use of the imaginary "Ben" to make her point. Would the professor get nosey and ask questions?

She pulled her handwritten notes from her backpack and typed them into a school computer.

I'm afraid I have to disagree with the author. She

wasn't talking about an inanimate object like a candy cane or coffee cup; she was talking about someone's life. And what got lost wasn't a set of keys or a sock; it was a person. Ignoring a painful past leads to more of the same.

Take Ben, a friend of mine with a traumatic childhood. He learned to lock things away—the insults, the slaps, and worse. "Stop your sniveling," he was told. "Don't be a baby. Tell, and you'll be sorry."

But bottling it up was like overfilling a dam with a thousand cracks. He had trouble sleeping, thoughts of suicide, and dreams of elaborate plots to exact revenge.

As unlikely as it may sound, Ben found the remedy in reliving his trauma. He cried about his life, punched a pillow, and screamed at the top of his lungs. He shared the nightmarish experiences he'd kept secret with a trusted friend, and only then could he allow in the positive energy required to build the better life he wanted.

Avoiding the truth can lead to consequences of disastrous proportions. The keys are facing the ugly truth and acting with intention.

She opened her notebook to a blank page and wrote: Find a trusted friend.

****

January 15, 2017— continued

With less than eight hours before returning to work, Julia glanced at her "Night Before Work" checklist. Select and hang work clothes in the bathroom. Stock baby bag (consult baby bag supply checklist). Lay Trey's clothes on changing table. Transfer six frozen breast milk bags to the fridge.

She slept three hours and woke up crabby.

Chapter Seven

January 16, 2017
The Cascade City Chronicle

"Ladies Fill Local ER After Eating Marijuana-Laced Brownies at Wine-Tasting Party"

Julia arrived at Kids' Korner, stepped out of the car, slung the diaper bag over her shoulder, pulled Trey out of his car seat, stopped mid-parking lot, and began shaking, paralyzed on the spot.

What if the staff burns him with overheated breast milk?

What if they don't give him enough tummy time, and he gets a flat head like the ancient Mayans who grew up with boards strapped to their noggins?

What if some giant-toothed toddler bites him?

She held him cheek to cheek and blubbered. "I don't know if I can do this. I want this, but I don't want this. Do you know what I mean? Of course, you don't know what I mean. You're a frickin' baby. I'm leaving you in this foreign place with strangers. Strangers who might have a habit of overheating breast milk. Please don't hate me."

A light-eyed young woman wearing a white sweatshirt with a dalmatian in a firefighter helmet approached. "Mrs. Navarro-Nilsson? I'm Cassandra. We saw you drive up. You've been standing out here for a while. Why don't you come in, and we'll get Trey settled."

Julia opened her purse and pulled out a tissue. "I'm a horrible mother," she said, blowing her nose.

Cassandra's mouth formed an O, and her eyes darted as if looking for someone to rescue her. "I'm sure that's not the case, Julia. May I call you Julia? You might feel nervous about leaving your baby at daycare; that's common with new moms. But it'll be all right, I promise. He'll be in good hands. You can call Betty or myself to ask how he's doing."

"But I love him."

Cassandra looked at Julia sideways like she was a cuckoo bird. "Of course, you love him—you're his momma. Now come inside."

Julia rocked him in a rocking chair in the corner of the infant room, where babies were cared for by Cassandra and Betty. Betty looked like a typical grandma you might see in a denture cream commercial, and for some reason, that made Julia feel a bit better. Her baby's daytime mom had white hair, clean fake teeth, and resembled the guy on the oatmeal box.

Cassandra took Trey, and Julia leaned in to kiss his chubby hand with the cute little dimples where his knuckles should be. "They're going to take good care of you," she reassured herself.

She bawled the moment she left the building, felt diarrhea coming on and her hands sweating. A lovely way to start the workday.

****

Julia walked up to Kelvin at the extended u-shaped desk with the phone system monitor, schedule, and the

39

day's newspaper for reference—a command center of sorts.

"Good morning," she said, looking splotchy-faced and miserable (but with empty bowels—hurray!).

Kelvin motioned to his headset, meaning he was on a call.

"Where's Carlton?" she mouthed.

"Vacation. You look like heck." He wrote on a large sticky note.

She pulled the notepad over and grabbed a dull pencil. Egads. Apparently, pencil-sharpening went by the wayside in her absence. "Thanks, friend," she wrote.

"Welcome back, Julia," Sistine, a twenty-something-year-old CSR said. She wore a white eyelet lace skirt, a tucked-in red blouse, a wide black belt, and a red-and-white pinstriped bow in her bobbed red hair. "I have a customer using words that wouldn't come out of a drunken sailor's mouth. You know I don't care for that kind of language." She set her hand on a jutted hip.

"You want me to take the call, like old times?" But Julia already knew the answer. She moved quickly to Sistine's workstation and slipped on the headset. "*Cascade City Chronicle*. My name is Julia. How can I help you this morning?"

"What happened to the dingleberry I was talking to?" the customer barked.

"She didn't care for your language, sir. I'm the manager. How can I help you?"

"I'll tell you how you can help me. Arrest my newspaper boy for stealing my girlfriend's shoes."

"How do you know the newspaper carrier stole your girlfriend's shoes?"

"Misty, that's my girlfriend. She jogs every morning

and leaves her running shoes on the porch outside our apartment door. They went missing yesterday. When the newspaper guy showed up this morning, I opened the door and caught the little shit red-handed—or red-footed, shall I say."

"And how do you know it was him who stole her shoes?"

"He was wearing 'em, bitch!"

****

Julia and Jerry ate lunch in the cafeteria—her a BLT with fries, a slice of chocolate cream pie, and a glass of whole milk, and him a chef salad with lemon and a side of water.

"Lookin' good, my friend. I like your baby blue glasses," she said. "Are they new? They complement your eyes."

Jerry pouted.

Julia slid low in her chair and dropped her chin. "I've missed you."

"Don't tell me that," he hissed. "I say bullshit. What is wrong with you? Do you know how many times I called? Didn't you listen to my messages? I texted you every day for a week. I thought you up and died or joined a convent or something."

"You know better than that. No convent would take me: too much cussing and a history of kinky sex in weird places. I thought about calling you back. Honest to God. I've just been a little—a little—down in the dumps."

Jerry, dressed in slim-fit jeans, a lavender and white-striped shirt, a deep purple blazer, and black Gucci loafers with no socks, lifted a white-blond eyebrow that matched his white-blond buzz cut.

"Okay, a lot down." Julia looked outside and

watched a bank of dark clouds slide in as if on a conveyor belt. "Turns out, motherhood's not exactly my thing. I'm always irritated and want nothing more than to get sucked into a black hole and disappear like—Amelia Earhart—or—or—obliterated by an asteroid like the dinosaurs. Am I allowed to say that? I'd rather disappear like Amelia Earhart than be a mother." She looked around to see if anyone had heard her.

"You're being awfully dramatic, darling."

"No, I'm *more* irritated than usual. I'm a motherhood flunky, Jer, and I've never flunked out of anything. I'm not perfect, but that hasn't kept me from trying my whole life. There was a time when I had my shit together. I solved tough problems, I made delicious dinners, I advocated for my employees, and plucked my chin hair. I don't even know where the tweezers are now." She wrinkled her eyebrows and ran her fingers along her chin.

"So, you were perfect before the baby? Is that what you're saying?"

"Hell, no. But I don't give a crap now. I've given up *trying* to be perfect. I feel lost—and, and—fatter than ever. You know those giant rolls of cinnamon roll dough they roll out behind the window at the mall? That's what the flub that hangs over my waistband looks like. Charlie and I barely talk except about the baby and the weather. I'm sure he's tired of having a sorry-ass wife who's not interested in sex anymore. He's getting…"

"Into porno?" Jerry slapped the table.

"It's not funny. I have a good job, a house, a wonderful husband, and a healthy baby—what's there to be sad about? I've gone *loca in la cabeza*. I'm serious. I don't know if I can do this."

"You're going to be fine, Julia. Give yourself a break. This is still new for you."

Easy for you to say, you childless twerp. "Forget it. I don't want to talk about it anymore. What have I missed around here?"

"Well, you would have known if you'd called me back." Jerry leaned in and put his finger to his lips. "The Kellers are in talks with Troy Media to sell *The Chronicle*."

"I knew it. Carlton sounded weird the last couple of times I talked with him." She picked up a stray piece of lettuce and stuffed it back into her sandwich. "Who or what is Troy Media?"

Jerry crossed his arms across his chest. "Oh, so you talked with that skirt-chaser and not me."

"Stick to the point. What's Troy Media, and why should I care, Jerry?"

"The Kellers are looking to sell the paper. The blowhards from Troy Media in Chicago don't give a rat's ass about little ole Cascade City. They're buying up radio stations and small to midsize newspapers to turn a quick buck. The list of newspapers on the obituary page keeps growing, and ours is next."

"Tell me you're kidding, Jerry," she whispered.

"Marcia from Finance is working the numbers behind the scenes—top secret stuff. I had to buy her two piña coladas at the Fiver-Diner to get her to spill her guts. God, that woman has breath that'd kill a horse. Even the rum didn't kill it."

Julia looked at her watch. "Damn, I gotta get back. Let's talk later."

"I'm not callin' you anymore. You call me!"

Julia grabbed a sheet of foil from the utensil area to

cover her sandwich and pie and then trotted up the stairs to the first floor.

****

"Hey," Julia said, taking a seat next to Kelvin. "Thanks for taking care of things while I was gone."

Kelvin fake-punched her arm. "Learned from the best."

"I haven't seen Carmen—the new hire."

"Supposed to start today, but she never showed."

"Seriously?" Julia's shoulders sagged. "She wanted this job real bad—that's the impression you got, too, right?"

Kelvin nodded. "Called here nearly every day until I offered her the job. I tried calling her last Friday to confirm her start time, but her number was disconnected. Weird."

Julia tapped her foot. "I have a bad feeling about this, Kelvin." She remembered Carmen's fingers wrapped in paper towels and tape. "I'm worried about her. There was a discrepancy with the home address—and now her phone's disconnected. How could someone who wanted the job so badly not show up or call? You think something bad could have happened to her? I hear alarm bells."

"I think ya should just let it be. Now that you're back, you can hire somebody else."

She returned to her desk and checked the manager intranet to see if any new CSR applications had come in. If she got on it, she could have someone hired and on board within a month. There were no CSR applications in the queue. Not surprising, considering she hadn't posted an ad for new positions in months. *You're it, Carmen Cooper. What's your story?*

Julia shuddered as a tingle ran up her spine.

****

The daily daycare report said: "Got through the day like a champ. Drank three to four ounces at eight forty-five a.m., eleven thirty a.m., and half past two. Napped twice at nine a.m. and one p.m., ninety minutes each. Two bowel movements. What a sweetie."

"Glad you were such a good boy at daycare," Julia told Trey as they pulled out of the parking lot. "You wanna do Mommy a huge favor and sleep ninety minutes at home? *Por favor*? Listen up, *mi corazón*. We're gonna take a little drive now, so behave yourself when we arrive. We have something important to look into." She entered an address in her phone's navigation system.

Six-six-eight-eight Overlook Drive, Cascade City

She drove along the water's edge and up a private road lined with giant rhododendron bushes—thick green perennials that formed a natural barrier to the road and the house next door. A palatial colonial-style home stood at the top of the hill with white columns and a circular drive.

Julia got out of the car and peeked into the backseat. Her little man's hands rested on his round belly, rising up and down with each sleeping breath.

"Who are you?"

Julia whirled around.

An aged Percy Booth stood on the porch—tall, straight-backed, full head of silver hair, sky-colored eyes, and a gold-handled revolver in his hand. "I don't take kindly to people who show up unannounced."

Chapter Eight

January 16, 2017— continued

Percy Booth, her father's Hollywood hero, looked at her sideways as if she were some barrel-chested, tattooed guy named Guido.

"Are you deaf? Who are you?" he demanded.

"I'm Julia Navarro-Nilsson from *The Cascade City Chronicle*. There's no need for that gun, Mr. Booth. Please. I have an infant in the car."

"I don't want the newspaper." He tightened his grip on the gun and pointed it at a plaque on the outside wall near the doorway. "Are you incapable of reading the 'No Solicitors' sign? I don't like reporters, and I sure as hell don't give interviews."

"Sir, I am not here to sell the paper and am not a reporter. Does Carmen Cooper live here? She was supposed to start work at *The Chronicle* today but didn't show up. I'm doing a welfare check."

"Papa?" came a voice from inside the house.

Booth looked over his shoulder with daggers in his eyes. "What is the meaning of this?"

Carmen stepped onto the front porch, dressed in gray sweatpants and a man's white T-shirt with grayish armpit stains. "Ms. Navarro-Nilsson? What are you doing here?"

"You were supposed to start today but didn't come in or call. Is everything all right?"

"I've been sick—with the stomach flu. And a bad headache."

"Why didn't you call?"

"I should have. I apologize, but I've—I've just been so sick."

"Do you still want to work for us?"

Carmen looked expectantly at the man she called 'Papa.'

"I can assure you; it won't happen again, Miss—Nelson, was it?" Booth responded. "Carmen will not be going to work—not tomorrow, the next day, or any day. She does not have my permission."

"Carmen can answer for herself," Julia said, feeling ballsy-terrified-empowered-like-she-might-wet-her-pants. "Carmen? You're a legal adult; technically, you don't need your father's permission."

"Carmen, go inside—now. I want to speak with Ms. Nelson alone," Booth said in a low growl. "And shut the door. I'll deal with you later."

Julia envisioned Carmen's damaged fingers wrapped in a sorry-ass splint and subconsciously put her hand to her throat.

Carmen shuffled inside and looked out one of the long narrow windows flanking the front door.

Booth descended the steps and stood an arm's length from Julia. "Before you get the hell off my property, I must offer a word of caution."

"I'm not interested in your word of caution, sir. It's getting late, and I have to get my son home."

"This will only take a moment, Ms. Nelson."

"It's Navarro-Nilsson."

"Does it matter? Now, you listen closely. Long ago, I lived a high-profile life. With it came an army of unwanted and unrelenting attention by the media, money-grabbers, backstabbers, and so-called admirers. I'm old and out of the limelight now, and that is by design. Uninvited visitors are not welcome here. *You* are not welcome here. If you show up again, I will consider you a dangerous intruder. The law protects a man who acts to defend his life and property. Do I make myself clear?"

Julia's stomach churned. "Fine. Now you listen to *me*, Mr. *Bath*," she seethed, with the best don't-screw-with-me-face, she could fake. "I don't like you and don't care how rich you are, who you know in high places, or even how much my father liked your movies, which are all boorish and sexist, in my opinion. Carmen came to *me* for a job, and I came here to speak with *her*, not you. You're…" She gulped. "… not very nice, and nothing says 'crazy old coot' like bringing a gun to the door when someone knocks. *And* it looks phony!"

Booth cocked the gun.

She took two steps back. "I have a mind to turn you in for threatening me."

Booth stood unfazed.

"You know what? This could make a good newspaper story—Hollywood Has-Been Threatens Woman and Baby."

Booth's chest puffed up. "Get off my property!"

Before putting the car in reverse, Julia looked toward Booth. Carmen held a piece of paper against the window. It read, "I'm sorry. Please, I need to work."

"Hell's bells. That was a close one," Julia told Trey, now awake and sucking noisily on his fingers. "Kelvin was right. Maybe I should have let this be." She paused. "Nah. Your momma's not one to let things be, *chiquito*. That girl's in trouble, and someone has to save her."

****

"Joanne!" she heard Papa Percy shout.

Carmen opened the door a sliver to look downstairs.

"Yes, señor?" her mother replied as she entered the foyer, drying her hands on a dishtowel.

Papa tightened his jaw. "Carmen took a job at the newspaper," he barked. "Did you know about this?"

"She deed what?" her mother asked. From Carmen's vantage point, she looked so small and frail in her pink housecoat and sandals, with the silver packing tape holding the heel strap together.

"Don't play dumb with me. She took a job at the newspaper. Are you saying you didn't know?"

"No, sir, I do not know. I tell her to queet thee job, okay? That what joo want? Plees, señor, she young ahn make a meestake."

"Of course, that's what I want. I shouldn't have let her go to college. I gave her an inch, and she took a mile." He glared at her mother, and then his face softened. "It's okay, Joanne. You're not in trouble. I'll be in Dorthea's room. Bring the whiskey."

He walked up the curved staircase to the double doors leading to his dead wife's room. Carmen closed her bedroom door quietly before he reached the final step.

****

Julia arrived home and fixed quesadillas for dinner. No vegetable or guacamole—just tortillas, taco meat, and cheese. "Side dishes are overrated," she told Charlie, remembering the fluffy Mexican rice and charro beans she used to serve.

"I'm adding pickled jalapeño slices to my quesadilla. Does that count as a side dish?" Charlie asked.

"Yesss." She pointed to the jar on the counter. "*That's* a vegetable, yes, indeed it is. You know, one of these days, I'll get back to making better meals, singing, knitting, and reading books. And taking a daily shower."

"Take your time, babe. No one's rushing you. And you smell fresh as a daisy to me."

"Daisies smell like poo, Charlie."

"Like I said."

Julia threw a crumpled paper towel at him.

They ate dinner at the card table masquerading as a dinette table, and she squeezed Charlie's hand. She contemplated whether to tell him about what happened with Percy Booth. *Percy Booth. A Hollywood movie star damn near tried to kill me. Well, he didn't exactly try to kill me, but he did stand on his big porch with a gun in his hand, looking flat-out evil. But it's over, and there's nothing Charlie can do about it now. Why stress him out? I'll tell Jerry. I don't care if I stress him out.*

****

Trey went down for the night. Or rather, he went down for his usual one to two hours. In the Navarro-Nilsson house, "down for the night" phraseology was nothing but folklore—more of a stretch goal—a dream state—a damn tease.

Charlie parked himself on the sofa with his laptop to do research for a paper titled "Aligning Technology Learning with Classroom Curriculum." Julia sat on the bench at the foot of their bed with the phone to her ear. And the bedroom door closed.

"He had a gun on him, Jerry," she whispered.

"What's Charlie think about all this? Is he going there to use those finely sculpted muscles to beat the guy to a pulp?"

"I didn't tell him. Besides, Charlie's a peace-loving teddy bear."

"Julia…"

"Why worry him? He's dealing with enough already."

"Did the old man ever *point* the gun at you?"

"No. What difference does that make? He held the thing and looked at me like some homicidal dude in a hockey mask."

"How could you tell how he looked if he was wearing a hockey mask?"

"Shut up, you blockhead. You know what I mean."

"Well, don't bother calling the cops. Holding a gun at his side didn't break any laws. But it could make a juicy story. I'll start digging into his past. Illicit affairs, illegal drug use, a collection of women's dirty underwear. Who knows what I'll find? I mean, the guy's a fucking legend."

"If Carmen shows up tomorrow, I'll see what I can find out. I'm worried about her, Jer. When Booth came onto that porch, I knew I had to help her."

"And how exactly will you do that?"

"I don't have a plan yet, but I'm gonna need your help, that much I know."

"Uh-huh. Hey, don't tell anyone else about the big story we're about to break. I want an exclusive."

"Big story, huh? Fine, fine. How is your new boyfriend—the attorney?"

"Juan Carlos? He's full of himself. I dumped him

like yesterday's seven-dollar coffee cup."

"What'd he do?"

"He called my glasses *retro*. And I didn't like how he looked when he said it."

"You dumped him for that?"

"He might as well have told me I'm *ancient*. He said they reminded him of Clark Kent. They're not even the same color as Clark Kent's."

"Clark Kent's a hunk-o-burnin' love. Think, umm— Henry Cavill, broad shoulders, abs of steel."

"He meant George Reeves from the 1950s TV show."

"Jerry, he's never heard of George Reeves. How old is Juan Carlos?"

"Twenty-six."

"You're fifty-seven, Jer. You *are* ancient to a twenty-six-year-old. Try looking in an upscale grocery store that sells organic quinoa for twenty bucks a bag instead of Prince Hairy's Banana Boy Bar. The *millennial* gays hang there. Do they even say 'hang' anymore? Christ, I can't keep up with young people's slang nowadays."

"You're twenty-five, Julia. Don't rub it in."

"Goodnight, Jerry."

"Remember to keep your trap closed about the Booth thing. It could be my big break."

"And where do I fit in?"

"You're the connection to Carmen, my dear. What could be more important than that?"

****

Julia walked into the kitchen, leaned over Charlie's chair from behind, and reached inside his shirt to run her hands across his smooth, muscular chest. He smelled of soap and sandalwood.

He swiveled around to face her. "Whoa, Nellie. What's this? An invitation?"

"Oh yes, sir, it 'tis," Julia said in her sexiest bad British accent. She bit her lower lip to keep from screaming. Her desire for sex equaled her desire for gangrene.

"An invitation to what? Can you be more specific?" Charlie undid the tie on her robe.

She shimmied her shoulders, the robe slid down her arms, and dropped to the floor.

"Oh, sweet Jesus," Charlie said as he kissed her belly button and deftly slid his hand between her thighs.

Chapter Nine

January 17, 2017
The Cascade City Chronicle

"Local Quilter Maurine Gunther Wins Quilters of America National Prize"

Carmen scooched herself into a sitting position against the wall. The neon green numbers on the clock glowed in the dark—five twelve a.m. The embarrassment from the incident with Julia sat in her gut like a hot stone, burning, burning. Once again, Papa Percy played the master puppeteer—said no to getting a job—that he didn't trust her—that he had ways to keep her in line. It would be college, home, and nowhere else. If she disobeyed, she and Mami would end up in Mexico, where someone, or a group of someones, wanted Mami dead. She wondered how much of the story was true—that Mami and Papi saw someone get killed—someone so important that the gang killed Papi to silence him and was still looking for Mami to do the same.

Her old diary might hold clues. She wrote all kinds of things in there.

Sixth Grade
May 28, 2009
Dear Monica,
You've probably been wondering where Ive been.

Well, I've been here all along but to sad to write. School is almost out and Jake Dixon wont talk to me anymore. I went to his house so we could do homework (in secret because Papa Percy would blow a gasket if he found out). Jake needs lots of help cuz he sees things backwards. His mom said hes to young to have a girlfrend but I am eleven and Jake is almost twelve. Lots of kids our age date each other. Its not like were going to make out or anything but I think about it sometimes!!! Would I keep my eyes open if he kissed me? Would I turn my head a little before the kiss? I wouldn't want our noses to hit. What if he stuck his tongue in my mouth? Gross. Gabby said she likes it and Joey Antonetti has a long tongue. Anyways Jakes mom doesn't like me. When she saw me at school she gave Jake the scary mom eyes. What did Jake do wrong? Or did I mess up? I said hello and how do you do. I need to wear cuter clothes. Jakes mom probably thought I dress like something the cat dragged in. Papa Percy says no when I ask for something so I dont ask for new clothes. Kids at school see my blue lunch card for poor kids and its so embarassing. Miss Montgomery says I am lucky to live in America but I was born here. Mami taut me a new song yesterday. She said its an old one called La Malagenya and its hard to sing but I dont mind. Anything I do with Mami is the best thing I do all day. We'll keep practicing because I don't have it memorized yet.

Anyways, after I got to Jake's house his Mom told me to go home.

****

January 17, 2017— continued

Julia glanced at the printer paper she hung on the refrigerator door.

"I have to stick to the program if I'm going to keep my head on straight," she told Charlie, pointing to the "Sanity Saver Schedule."

Six o'clock a.m.—get up

Six o-five a.m.—shower

Six twenty a.m.—get dressed (clothes laid out the night before)

Six twenty-five—make coffee

Six thirty a.m.—feed & dress Trey, *stock baby bag for daycare, move the bag to the front door, don't forget to move the baby bag

Five-minute cushion

Seven o'clock a.m.—leave for work

Seven fifteen a.m.—daycare drop-off

Seven thirty-five a.m.—walk the call center floor, greet CSRs

*two changes of clothes, two bottles, six bottle liners, two bibs, baby socks, booties, diaper cream, onesies, one short-sleeve and one long-sleeve, light blanket, burp cloth, diaper pad, six diapers, the puffy jacket that makes Trey look like a twelve-pound blue marshmallow, hat, four nursing pads, pkg diaper wipes, pkg baby booger wipes

"Jerry says you can plan for eighty percent of your life, and shit's just gonna happen for the other twenty."

"You agree with that?" Charlie asked.

"No way, José. Some people live on the fly. I plan, I use checklists, and I get shit done. "

"Good for you." Charlie kissed the tip of her nose. "Have I told you how much I love you lately?"

"Not since yesterday."

"How remiss of me." Charlie lifted her hair and kissed her neck. "I love you." He opened a hall door and bounced down the steps toward the basement garage.

She trotted after him. "I love you, too," she shouted into the stairwell. Charlie honked his car horn twice in response.

The "shit's just gonna happen" portion of her day started soon after he left.

Not part of the program: kitchen cabinet, barren of coffee

Not part of the program: an espresso stand stop (eight minutes)

Not part of the program: niggling feeling that something got left behind

Not part of the program: baby bag *not* in fucking car

Not part of the program: a drive home to retrieve stupid effing baby bag

Not part of the program: run through the house to get the piece of shit stupid ass baby bag

Not part of the program: a return to the car with Trey sitting in greenish-brown poop slime, which shot out his ass and onto the car seat in the twenty seconds she was gone.

"Jerry had it right. Shit's gonna happen," she mumbled as she pulled off Trey's poopy clothes, spreading rotting avocado-colored, ghastly-smelling goo all over the changing table pad, up his back, and in his hair. She gagged and dropped the tiny jeans and red T-shirt into the garbage and took the poop-proliferator into the bathroom to wash him up.

Not part of the program.

****

She made it through the employee entrance at eight o-two a.m., irritated as all get out. "Twenty-seven minutes off schedule," she grumbled as she made her way to the water cooler. Her mind wandered, which it did more and more often. The "forgetful baby brain" she had when she was pregnant hadn't gotten the memo that the baby had exited the premises.

She stewed about leaving Trey with caregivers who had other babies to care for, one teacher to every four babies.

He'll never get the personal attention that he deserves.

He could cry without anyone to pick him up because some other baby cries first.

He could have a wet diaper with no one to change him because one lady is on a break, and the second one's wiping poop slime off another little stinker.

Would Trey be better off at an in-home daycare with one caregiver?

But what if that singular caregiver turns out to be a couch potato who watches soap operas while Trey eats a watch battery?

What if a delivery guy steps on Trey while carrying a heavy object into the house?

Or drops a washing machine on him?

Or if the family dog, the victim of a rabid squirrel attack, bites him? Gah!

A million things could go wrong at an in-home daycare. There'd be no one else but the couch potato to keep a watchful eye on my precious little one—the one I thought I wanted, the one who came from Charlie's and my undying love for one another, or at least our horndog urges the day my egg dropped at the same time his sperm, like a heat-seeking missile, found its target. I'm pretty sure it was the day we drove up to Mount Rainier and pulled off the road to have a fu…

Water spilled over the top of her water bottle and splashed on her foot. "Hell's bells." She yanked a long section of stiff brown paper towels from the dispenser.

"Nice move, my little *cucaracha*." Carlton stood in the doorway wearing brown pants riding below his belly, a wrinkled long-sleeved yellow shirt, and a paisley polyester tie that landed above his navel. "Clean that up and come into my office."

"Do you even know what *cucaracha* means?"

"Of course not."

"It means cockroach, you cockroach," she said.

****

Carlton leaned back in his squeaky office chair. A mummified African violet and a carton of cigarettes sat on the file cabinet. A candy wrapper and an empty potato chip bag peeked out between old newspapers spread topsy-turvy across his desk.

"Don't tell anyone what I'm about to tell you, or your ass is grass. You promise?" The corners of his mouth turned upward like a sneaky cat with some furry thing between its jaws.

"Well, I don't want a grassy ass, so…"

"The Kellers are looking to sell *The Chronicle* to Troy Media. Newspapers can't turn a buck these days with the internet, the radio stations, and damn near everyone stealing newspaper content without paying a dime. And ad revenue's shrunk by seventy percent. If and when the Kellers sell, and I think they will, the call center's going somewhere labor's cheap, like Mumbai or the Philippines."

Jerry was right. Again.

Carlton reached for a pack of cigarettes. "All the papers are doing it—outsourcing the unskilled workers.

59

The papers that are left anyway."

"And? Are you telling them why they should keep us? Our budget is tiny compared to other departments. We're the public relations department without the public relations pay. And CSRs are not *unskilled*. Good customer service takes skills. It takes a high emotional intelligence many of our *executives* don't have."

Carlton wiggled his finger in his ear to satisfy an itch.

"Say something," Julia said. "Aren't you upset about this situation?"

"You see now why I wanted you back at work? Someone's gotta do all the laying off and move the work overseas. It's not gonna affect me. Me and Bessie have discussed it. Why should I hang around for the carnage? It's time to retire."

Poor Bessie. She married a guy with the last name Cressey. Bessie Cressey. And the guy was Carlton, who smelled of butt crack.

"Listen up, Julia. Some senior managers are going to Killian's this Friday at six o'clock. Wanna join us? We can talk more about it then, but you need to loosen up first."

"Trey's at daycare all day, and I don't want to miss more time with him." Julia felt a headache coming on. *He's retiring, and when I finally have a chance for promotion, the Kellers sell the paper.*

"Oh, right, the ankle-biter. Don't let the kid ruin your career, my little jal-uh-peeno. Between your position and mine, mine is the only one they'll keep. Someone's gotta manage the contractor in Manila or wherever. You're gonna have to keep distractions to a minimum if you wanna get ahead. And try wearing a Vneck, for God's sake. Cleavage matters in the hiring game."

"Don't associate the ankle-biter with my career. And leave my cleavage out of it. Plus, who says women can't do both? They do it all the time. I'm doing it now." *Badly*. "Come on, Carlton. Make this your legacy. Don't let them outsource us. Make sure they know how important we are—how much value we bring."

"Correction. *You* let leadership know how important we are. I'm as good as gone."

"I'll cut the recognition budget and employee development. Office supplies. I can cut back on office supplies. Fuckity fuck." She closed her eyes and pressed her fingertips to her forehead. "Since you won't help, should I go to Bob Keller directly?"

"Bennet Keller's running the show now. Bob's old as the hills." He stuffed a cigarette between his lips. "You think you have my position in the bag, but don't get ahead of yourself, *Mamacita*. They might keep you on long enough to lay all these people off, then show you the door. I suggest you prioritize getting your very fine derriere to Killian's and schmooze with upper management. And smile. You're too fucking serious."

"How long before you retire?"

"Until my backfill starts; a month max. Me and Bessie got our first vacation to Palm Beach planned already. I heard they have a good disco scene there. You don't know how good a dancer I am."

"Ugh."

****

Julia sat in her car and called Charlie. It went straight to voicemail. "Hey, babe, call me when you get a chance. It's not an emergency, and it's not about Trey.

Something's up at work. Love you."

Teaching took one hundred percent of Charlie's attention, and he rarely answered calls, ate lunch, or made it to the "adult/teacher bathroom" during school hours. The guy had a bladder the size of New Hampshire.

She went inside and found Kelvin in the hall on his way back to the call center.

"Carmen's here," he said.

"Oh, Lord. This'll be interesting. Where is she now?"

"In the conference room next to payroll. I'm on my way now."

****

One of the flickering fluorescent tube lights emitted a low-level buzzing sound, a warning that it was about to burn out. She'd add it to her long "Shit To Do" checklist. Carmen and Kelvin sat at a round table, Kelvin with a laptop and Carmen with an open three-ring binder, two highlighter pens, and a mechanical pencil.

"Good afternoon. How's it going in here?" Julia asked.

"We've been at it for an hour or so," Kelvin replied. "I'll take Carmen to the cafeteria for a break soon, and then we'll tour the buildin', includin' the loadin' dock and the pressroom." He turned to Carmen. "Sound good?"

"Yes, yes, of course," she said, watching Kelvin with big eyes and a slightly parted mouth. Julia recognized "the look." Most women couldn't help but notice him. Even the guys looked twice. At six feet four inches with broad shoulders, camel hump biceps, narrow hips, a sweet Southern drawl, and a gentleman's manner any mother would love, who wouldn't?

"Kelvin, when you get back, have Carmen stop by my desk. We need to chat."

"Fine and dandy. Carmen, ya wanna take that break now? I wouldn't mind a bit to eat myself. We can take it slow," he said. "Or do ya want me to getcha somethin' from downstairs and bring it back?" He chuckled. "I'd carry ya, but there's probably some safety policy against that."

Julia watched them walk away; only Carmen didn't walk so much as limp.

****

Carmen sat next to Julia's desk with a carton of orange juice in her hand. She signaled toward a spot on the desk. "May I set it there?"

"Let me put something down first," Julia replied, reaching for a coaster she kept in a drawer. "Here you go." She set it square with the desk's edge. "Welcome to *The Chronicle*, Carmen. Given what happened yesterday, I wasn't sure if I'd see you again. You can imagine how—how *unsettling* your father's behavior was."

Carmen crossed and uncrossed her legs. "I apologize for Mr. Booth's rudeness. He's not my father."

"Oh? You called him Papa Percy."

Carmen shuddered. "A figure of speech."

That's a bizarre figure of speech. "I see. During your interview, you said you didn't stay in touch with Percy Booth." Julia waited. Carmen had some explaining to do. The background noise of CSRs carrying on conversations filled the silence. "After you left, I looked up his address and saw that it was the same as yours. You lied during the interview."

"Please forgive me." Carmen sipped her orange

juice and then stared at the floor. "It's an unusual arrangement with Mr. Booth, and I didn't think it mattered where I live anyway. Please don't fire me."

"Where you live doesn't matter, but lying on your application does, Carmen. You also didn't show up on your first day of work or call. I could easily justify terminating you, but I will overlook it, okay? You're on probation for the first six months, and I can let you go for any reason within that period without notifying the unión. Do you understand?"

"Yes, ma'am. I can't lose this job. I'll do better, I promise."

"Can I ask why you're limping?"

Carmen opened her mouth as if to answer, then closed it again.

"I want to help, Carmen. That is if you want me to," Julia continued.

"I missed a step at school. I must be the clumsiest person in the world."

Chapter Ten

January 18, 2017
The Cascade City Chronicle

"Café Owners Martin and Bridget Beach Welcome Twins Rocky and Sandy"

While the antidepressant dulled her irritation, Julia still wanted to run away and become someone else. Such as: "Cecile Charbonneau," an unmarried French artist and violinist she invented, who, in her daydreams, lived in a baroque-style building with views of Notre Dame, used a million dots and specs to create stunning paintings a la George Seurat, ate nothing but cheese and bread and salami and buttery pastries and gelato, and never got tubby. Ahhh, if only she could be Cecile Charbonneau— with her endless pastries and gelato and no obligations to anyone. And zero body fat or low back hair.

"I wish we didn't have to go to work," she told Charlie, still lounging in bed with the covers up past her breasts as Charlie pulled his slacks on over his tight little ass, glanced in the dresser mirror, and pushed his thick blonde hair off his forehead.

"You and me both."

"Charlie?"

"Yeah?"

"I left you a message yesterday while you were in

class—about work." She straightened Charlie's pillow.

"Oh, darn. Sorry about that, babe. I completely forgot. One of my students ran down the hall with a pencil in his nose. He and his buddies thought it was hysterical until he tripped over his shoelace and smacked his face on the floor. What's going on with work?"

"Wait, hon. How is the kid?"

"The pencil punched a hole into the back of his mouth. He'll have to see an ear, nose, and throat doc. So what's this about work?"

"The Kellers are looking to sell *The Chronicle*, and Carlton is retiring."

"They started the paper more than a hundred years ago. What happened to 'pride in family ownership'? That's their big thing, isn't it?"

"They've been losing money for a long time, like every other newspaper worldwide."

"What about your job?"

"If they outsource us, they'll only need one manager to oversee the contractor. With Carlton gone, I can't imagine they'd hire someone else. I'm running the show mostly by myself as it is. It'd be an upgrade, honey—with a pay increase."

"*Not* that it'll happen, but what if you *don't* get Carlton's job?"

"Become the synchronized swimmer I always wanted to be?" *Except it would require wearing a bathing suit. In front of other people. Egad.*

Charlie laughed. "We'll figure it out if and when we need to. But honestly, I have complete faith that you'll get the promotion."

They hugged for a long time, her head tucked away in the hollow between his neck and shoulder—one of her favorite spaces in the world—warm, reassuring, and safe. Plus, he smelled good. The man oozed sweet-smelling goodness.

"I'll get us some dinner on my way home," Charlie said. "And please, don't worry—we'll handle whatever comes our way."

Julia nodded. "Happy Anniversary to you, too," she said, kissing his pillowy lips.

Maybe the deal with Troy Media won't happen.

And maybe shit-eating gorillas will replace dogs as America's favorite pets.

****

Jerry and Julia stood by the loading dock, wrapped in winter coats. *The Chronicle* trucks were out delivering papers to the delivery centers, where the carriers would roll them up with the day's advertising and stick them in plastic sleeves. Broken plastic straps used to keep newspaper bundles together, fast-food hamburger wrappers, a french-fry carton, and dozens of cigarette butts littered the ground.

Jerry lit an unfiltered clove cigarette. "What information did you get from Carmen?"

"Nothing yet, but she's limping. It's obvious she's in trouble. What if I call nine-one-one and report it anonymously?"

"And tell them what? That she's limping? No, we need to know more. And I've already done some research."

Julia blew warm air into her cold hands. "What kind of research?"

"The newsroom has access to secret sources." He exhaled a wispy plume of smoke.

"What secret sources?"

67

"An internet fan page called 'Booth's Boosters.' And a website called 'Hollywood Hounds.' Did you know the new rap sensation Biggie Lipz got butt implants? They install them through your butt crack. Can you believe it? Maybe they should start calling her Plumpie Rump or Stack-a-Crack."

"Do not comment on women's body parts, okay?"

"Yeah, yeah, okay. So, here's the lowdown. Percy Booth was born in Hinsdale, Illinois, in 1938, just outside Chicago. He moved to Los Angeles in 1959, hoping to make it big. After landing a few jobs in commercials and modeling for King Ranch Cigarettes, he made his first movie, *Montana Wild*, in 1960, which got him noticed by Hollywood's big producers. And I'm not surprised. Have you seen the studio photos of him back then? The guy was a fucking stud."

"Have you told your editor you're digging around a Hollywood hunk's past?"

"You think I'm some kinda fool? Any investigative work has to stay under wraps." Jerry looked down his nose over his glasses. "Marcus would never approve—he's a by-the-book kind of editor. Everyone's got to stay in their lane. The guy has no imagination whatsoever." Jerry reached inside his jacket and pulled a reporter's notebook out. "And speaking of studs. Did you notice my new stud? Diamond stud, that is." He touched his earlobe.

"Where'd you get that?"

"Juan Carlos," he said. "We're back together. They're going to make him a partner at his firm—the youngest partner in the firm's history, *and* he's gorgeous, *and* he's got a tongue piercing."

"That's great, Jer. I'm happy for you. What else did

you find out about Booth?"

"He married Yvonne Means in 1960, Samantha Alder in 1964, Valerie Hicks in 1970, and Dorthea Simms in 1975. They were married until she died in 1997—no kids of his own but one stepson, Stanford Simms, from Dorthea. Booth moved to Cascade City in 1995. I could find no criminal history, but I'll keep digging." Jerry took a long drag from his cigarette and snuffed it out with the heel of his clunky black ankle boot. "I was hoping for a criminal history."

"He could be engaged in criminal activity now; only we can't prove it yet."

"Exactly. I hope the guy's a drug lord or selling arms to the Afghans—or worse. What's he doing to Carmen? Is he her pimp?"

"Or hitting her in a kneecap with a baseball bat? I'll talk to her again and see if she says anything we can use—after I figure out how to save the paper, protect my employees' jobs, and get a promotion. And get a decent night's sleep at least three nights in a row." She rubbed her hands together and shivered. "And lose twenty pounds without exercising or blending green leafy shit into protein shakes. And avoid drinking protein shakes."

"Sure, and while you're at it, can you make sure no one cuts the entertainment and lifestyle reporter position?"

"Of course. I'm Wonder *Mujer*. No. That sounds dumb. I'm Wonder *Chica*. Hmmm." She tapped her finger on her chin. "Wonderella. It's perfect."

"What's perfect?"

"Wonder. Ella. Ella means 'she' in Spanish. Am I brilliant or what?"

"You're trying too hard, Wonderella. Let's go

inside." Jerry drew his coat collar in tightly around his neck.

"Fine, but I think the world needs a Latina superhero who kicks ass and takes names."

"*Si, señora.*"

The wind picked up and blew the cigarette butts across the ground in swirly circles. Jerry grabbed Julia's hand, and they ran inside.

****

Gertie Jackson, sporting a large-flowered print dress and newly dyed, thinning raspberry-red hair, peeked inside the cubicle walls.

"Hi, Julie," she began.

"Hi, Gertie. You know it gets my panties in a twist when you call me 'Julie.' Think of it as Julie-uh, with a U and an H at the end, if you must. I don't call you 'Ger,' do I? Now, what can I do for you?"

"I'm not feelin' too good. I'd like to leave early, but I'm outta sick pay. You think I can get an advance on my paycheck? Please? You gotta help me. The power company shut off our electricity, and everything in the fridge spoiled. My kids are sleepin' in their coats at night."

Julia held up her hands. "I'm sorry, Gertie. I've raised this question with payroll before. The answer is 'no.' If they did it for you, they'd have to do it for everyone who asked, and people from the call center show up at the payroll window asking for an advance more often than you know. I wish I could get you guys better pay. But your union and the company have to negotiate that in your next contract."

"Okay," Gertie said quietly. "I'll try to stick it out. I'm just tired and a little out of breath. I'm sure it's nothin'. My shift's over in a few hours. Thanks anyways."

"Hey, Gertie?" Julia fished through her wallet. "I know it's not much." She held out a twenty-dollar bill, the only cash she had besides a few coins.

"You're so sweet, Julie." Gertie's eyes filled with tears as she stuffed the money in her bra. "I'll pay you back; I promise."

Julie-UH had heard that before. Rarely did she see the money again. Part-time work at low pay meant some CSRs had to choose between paying their electric bill or buying their kid's asthma medication. What a job—getting yelled at by subscribers all day, irregular hours, plus weekend work for a measly paycheck.

****

Two hours later, Natalia from purchasing appeared in Julia's cubicle.

"Julia, you've gotta come quick," Natalia said breathlessly. "One of your employees is sick."

Julia jumped up and followed her.

****

Gertie's wide feet in purple flats showed under the second gold bathroom door in a row of four. "Gertie, what's wrong?" Julia's heart pounded like a double-time bass drum.

"It's like an elephant's sittin' on me, and my jaw hurts," she said.

"I'm calling nine-one-one. Hold on."

"No!"

"No? What are you talking about? I have to. You could be having a heart attack."

"Julie—you gotta pull up my panties before they get here."

Julia ran out the door, told Natalia to make the call, and ran back. "*What* is it that you want me to do, Gertie?"

"I'm gonna open the door—and you gonna come in and pull up my panties. I'm beggin' you. Don't let 'em see me like this."

Gertie, five feet two inches and three hundred pounds, fumbled with the latch on the door. Her white nylon panties stretched between her ankles.

"Oh, hell's bells, Gertie. How am I going to do this?" Julia bent over. "You're going to be okay; the paramedics are coming."

"I'm so sorry, Julie. I'm sweatin' all over."

Right then and there, Julia decided that anyone on a toilet seat, mid-heart attack, had permission to call her "Julie."

She put one arm under Gertie's armpit and tried to lift her enough to slide her panties up and over her right hip. She strained so hard she prayed that her nervous stomach and anal sphincter were up to the challenge. Gertie's panties didn't move an inch. Two tries later, Julia gave up.

"What am I gonna do if I can't work?" Gertie whispered. "I can't pay my bills as it is. Maybe you should cancel the nine-one-one call. I'll be okay. Phone calls gotta be pilin' up with me gone."

"Paramedics," announced a muscly, dark-haired dude with a horseshoe mustache and a chin dimple large enough to house a vertical pinkie finger.

"My panties are down," Gertie said to the mustache and his equally hunky coworker.

Dimple-man flashed Julia a quizzical look as she backed out of the stall, still stooped over from yanking on Gertie's skivvies.

72

"She wants her panties pulled up," Julia said. "Sorry, Gertie. I ran out of time. You're going to be okay. These fine gentlemen will take good care of you."

"Call—my son—Nate," she answered, breathlessly. "He'll have to—pick up—his brothers and sisters at—school."

****

Julia sent Gertie a gift basket she couldn't afford. A hundred and seventy-nine bucks for some lemon shortbread, apples, pears, baklava, fig and olive crackers, truffles, and cheese. Shit. She should have put it together herself, but where on God's green earth would she have found the time? Between work, Trey, and the house, she barely had time to do the laundry or pluck her eyebrows, which were starting to look like a fuzzy black caterpillar squatting on her face.

She worried about her employees. Gertie recovering from a heart attack and no money for her electric bill. Monty, a gentle pothead who lived in his 1981 banged-up, loaded-with-crap sedan, came in most nights to forage through garbage cans for food. Susannah, an employee with Raynaud's disease, had one leg amputated below the knee as a teen. The other needed to come off, but her religion forbade blood transfusions. *What if she needs it to save her life?*

And, of course, Carmen, living with a gun-toting, baseball bat-carrying movie star. *Is he her father? Or her lover? Why does she stay with him? Should I get her out of there? How can I get her out of there? What will happen if I do?*

****

Charlie got stuck at school with an overbearing parent haggling over his perfect child's spelling test score.

"What's to haggle over?" Julia said into her phone. "The kid either spelled the word right or he didn't."

"His son spelled belief 'b—e—l—e—a—f.' "

"A future environmentalist. Get it? Be leaf?"

"That's funny 'cause the dad owns a chemical company."

Julia opened the refrigerator and peered inside. "All we've got is moldy cheese at home. If you order dinner from Mama Mendoza's, I'll pick it up."

"Works for me."

****

The restaurant had eighteen tables on red and black indoor-outdoor carpet squares. Hand-painted velvet art depicting a bullfighter, a Spanish dancer in full regalia with a white lace fan, and Mexican beer posters hung on the walls. Colorful sugar skulls lined the counter behind the bar. Two taxidermy frogs played pool on a wooden stand by the cash register.

Steam wafted through the kitchen window and into the seating area. The scent of seasoned ground beef, tortillas on the griddle, beans cooked with ham hock, and garlic took her back to her childhood in south Texas. Aunts, uncles, cousins, and friends ate, drank beer with lime, and sang in multiple-part harmony until after dark with her papá on guitar—some of her life's most magical moments.

The restaurant owner, Ana Mendoza, looked as stunning as ever in a flowy black skirt embroidered with vines, leaves, and colorful birds, a white cotton blouse with short puffy sleeves, and dangly turquoise earrings. Her silver hair sat atop her head in a tight bun with a turquoise and white abalone butterfly comb on one side.

"*Hola*, Julia." Ana kissed Julia on both cheeks. "How are you?" She looked down at Trey in his car seat. "*Aye, qué hermoso*. What's his name?"

Julia foisted the car seat onto a booth table nearby. "His name is Trey, but his full name is Charles Arthur Nilsson III, 'Trey' for short," she answered in Spanish, thankful to have someone to practice with.

Ana wrinkled her nose. "Teenagers will push his head in a toilet with a name like that. You feed him plenty of serrano peppers, you hear me? Make him grow lots of hair on his chest."

"Fine, Ana, but you named your son 'Dagoberto,' and I have seriously mixed feelings about that. On a different subject, have you heard of Percy Booth?"

Ana threw her hand up in the air. "Of course."

"What's he like? I mean, have you ever talked to him?"

"Hush now." Ana scanned the area. "Come over here where we can talk freely." She led Julia to a small table near the back. "Why do you want to know about Booth? As a general rule, I don't share information about my customers. Some say the most astonishing things here, but I'm discreet, as you would expect from a woman of my standing in the community."

"This isn't a doctor's office, Ana, and you don't have a confidentiality agreement with the man. One of my employees, a young woman, eighteen years old, lives with him, and something's not right; she's scared of him, for sure. And he's a loose cannon which I know from personal experience."

"What do you mean?"

"Let's just say he and his revolver had a run-in with me at his home."

"Mr. Booth is older than me—maybe in his seventies. Then again, who's to say older people can't have lovers? And Booth would be a real catch—still handsome as the devil and loaded. He lives in a huge house on a hill." Ana rubbed her thumb and fingers together, the universal sign of money.

"No, no; I didn't say they were *lovers*. Or at least I *hope* they're not lovers—that would be beyond ghastly. Him in his seventies and her in her teens?"

"So, what are you talking about?"

"There's something odd going on, and I want to know what it is."

"Perhaps a sugar daddy, then? Like, no sex, just someone beautiful to keep him company and take to fancy occasions. Mr. Booth and Senator Mathis are regulars here. They come in for lunch every Friday at noon and sit at the same table in the farthest corner of the room. We use it to fold napkins but clear it off before they arrive."

"A senator in Cascade City?"

"*Aye*, Julia. For someone who works at a news organization, you don't know much. He's the retired senator from Florida, Emerson Mathis—the man who fought the city on building restrictions for his obscenely large house. He looks at me like he's starving, and I'm a platter of fajitas. And I kind of like it." Ana bit her lower lip and gave her hips a little shake. "I'm hard to resist. Although Emerson's short and stocky with a bowling ball for a head and no neck. I ignore him as best I can without being rude. I treat my clients with the utmost respect—neck or no neck."

A young man dressed in black walked to the table, holding two white paper bags.

"Thank you, Alberto," Ana said, grabbing the bags and handing them to Julia. "Alberto, another perfectly good boy's name. Masculine. Your son won't go anywhere in life with a name like '*Tree*.' "

Julia ignored the jab about Trey's name. "Did Charlie pay for this?"

"Yes, it's all done."

"Thanks for everything." Julia pressed a five-dollar bill into Ana's hand. "Extra tip for Alberto. And, please, let me know if you hear anything juicy from Booth the next time he comes in here."

"Of course. We Latinas must stick together, but this is a special arrangement. I don't spread gossip as a regular practice. Speaking of which, did you hear that Gabriella Winston is filing for divorce? I knew she was a gold digger from the start. Her husband's old as the hills with a load of east coast money."

Julia arched her eyebrows. "But you don't spread gossip."

"Of course not." Ana walked away, chin in the air.

Julia left with Trey, still in his car seat. When she locked it into its backseat base, he smiled at her, and her heart felt warm and gooey and maybe even maternal for the first time since he arrived on the scene.

Chapter Eleven

January 18, 2017— continued

Carmen heard three faint taps on the bedroom. "Mami, is that you?" she asked.

"*Sí, Mija,*" came the weary voice on the other side.

"Come in," Carmen said, sitting against the wall with a copy of her assigned reading, Martin Luther King's "Our God is Marching On" speech given in Montgomery, Alabama.

Her mother, Consuelo Camacho, aka Joanne Cooper—the fake name they gave her when she crossed the border, came into the room wearing a white Mexican housedress with red embroidery around the neck and gray quilted slippers, one of which had a peek-a-boo hole for a stocking-covered toe. Her cropped hair, a mix of charcoal black and silvery ash, fell just below the ears— a no-fuss style perfect for a woman who never left the confines of the house.

"Why did you arrive so late? Your classes finished five hours ago," Mami asked.

"I'm tired, Mami, and I have a lot of homework," Carmen replied, nodding at the papers in her hands. "I'd love to talk with you, but can we do it tomorrow?" Carmen grabbed Mami's velvety-soft hand and held it against her cheek. A cuff-like black and blue bruise covered Consuelo's thin wrist. "He's a monster, and I hate him," Carmen seethed.

"Never mind that." Consuelo pulled her hand away. "He said you took a job at the newspaper." She closed the door. "It made him very angry with me."

"If I keep the job, I'll have at least two thousand dollars in my bank account a year from now. That could be enough to hire an attorney—or at least, I think so. I've never hired an attorney before."

Red splotches appeared on Consuelo's face and neck. "You will do no such thing."

"You don't want to live like this forever, do you? I want a job—a real one," pleaded Carmen. "I want to get married and have a family—and friends. What are we going to do? Wait until he dies? He could live another ten years. I know this could turn out bad, but how else can I get us out of here? I have to take a chance. And so do you."

Consuelo made the sign of the cross. "Is someone at the college putting ideas into your head? Have you told anyone about our lives here?"

"*Aye*, Mami. I'm going to get us out of here. Look at your wrist. Don't you want to fight back? If not for yourself, for me?"

Consuelo held a finger to her lips and glanced at the door. "He could be in Dorthea's room next door."

Carmen grabbed two tissues from the nightstand, one for her and the other for her mother. "I'll tell him I quit the job, okay?"

"You will *tell* him that you quit, or you will quit? I pray that you make the right decision. Don't do anything you're going to regret, Carmen. Where would we go if we left? And what would we live on? We don't have enough money to be on our own. It's not that bad here. We're in America, away from—the narcos that killed your father. Mr. Booth provides us with food and shelter. Isn't that enough?"

"No."

Consuelo bent her head and touched her mouth to her clasped hands. "Hail Mary, full of grace…"

****

Carmen opened her diary. She had another reckoning with her past.

Seventh Grade

January 4, 2010

Dear Monica

Its the first day back to school from X-Mas break. Mami croshayed me a hat and scarf same as two years ago. Lizzie got a camera and knee high boots and a phone and Emory got a real electric guitar, headphones and a keyboard and recording equipment. She's gonna be famous one day. She said I could be her manager. Papa Percy doesn't get me a present because I'm not his kid. Papi would have gotten me the present I wanted like a flat-screen tv but he died before I was born. Lizzie and Emory had sleepovers over vacation and Papa Percy wouldn't let me go. I can't go anywhere not even birthday parties. I wanna play soccer like Emory. I wanna take piano lessons like Kaitlyn. Why are there so many girls named Kaitlyn and Caitlyn and Kate and Katie and Caitee and Katy? I'm the only beaner in my class. The kids call me Beanie. I don't like it but I keep my mouth shut. I can't cause any trouble. Mami made me promise. Anyway I never get what I want. Papa Percy has a tv in his room but he locked me in Dortheas room after he caught me watching it. Creepy dead lady. He locks me in there all the time. I wish he were dead. Mami said I should be grateful to him. Why should I be grateful?

Your friend,
Carmen

****

"Carmen! Get down here," Booth shouted.

Carmen put the diary in its hiding place and walked to the top of the stairs.

"Yes?" she shouted, her voice echoing off the walls of the two-story entryway.

"Come here. Now."

She walked down the spiral staircase, stopping on the final step. A commanding six feet two inches tall, Booth stood on the white marble floor in his silky black pants and a dark green smoking jacket with black satin lapels. A 1920s Venetian crystal chandelier hung overhead—a useless decoration since it and most of the other lights in the house seldom got turned on.

"Have you quit the job?" he demanded. "I don't want that fool woman coming over here again."

"I…"

"I am not finished. If that woman from *The Chronicle* shows up, I will enact my right to protect myself from a would-be intruder. And you will be responsible. Do you get my meaning?"

"Yes, sir. I already quit the job. She won't come here again. But can I please have your permission to stay at the library some nights? I need the computers for homework. If I had a laptop, I wouldn't need to…"

"No laptop. You bring one in here, and the FBI will infiltrate the house—the phones, the TV, even the coffee maker. I've said this before. The government keeps tabs on people like me—actors, musicians, all of us. And for good reason. Some of them are spies for governments I don't care to name. Not me. I love my country, unlike you and *your* kind, flooding our borders and expecting handouts." He stood up and closed the blinds. "Never leave these open. We can't take any chances."

"Okay. What about the library at school?"

"I'll permit the library, but you are to come straight home afterward. No job. No visitors. School and home. That's it. You screw this up, and I'll lock you away for a week. Without meals." He smirked. "A person can survive a long time without food."

"Yes, sir."

Booth headed toward his recliner in the den, where he listened to cowboy music by Gene Autry, Bing Crosby, and Johnny Cash. "Get me a drink."

Carmen pretended she didn't hear him.

Chapter Twelve

January 19, 2017
The Cascade City Chronicle

"National Chain Green Goddess SuperMart to Replace Family-Owned Cherry-on-Top Grocery Long-Time Residents In Mourning"

Julia woke up at six in the morning feeling like she'd gone ten rounds with a world-champion boxer.

Body sensation: every muscle—aching

Right breast: hot to the touch with a pink streak descending from the nipple, approximately three inches in length

Fever: one hundred and two degrees

Energy level: a half-step up from dead

Mindset: what the fuck *is* this?

Charlie left earlier than usual to prepare lesson plans on climate zones. If he'd been home, he could have brought Trey to her. Instead, she dragged herself into the nursery, changed the little guy's diaper, laid him in her bed, kissed his warm cheek, and popped her left breast in his mouth.

A searing lightning-strike pain shot through her the moment he clamped down.

She screamed.

He screamed.

It took five minutes for them both to stop screaming.
"I think you had something to do with this, *chiquito*.
Thank you very much." Her tears flowed like tiny rivers.

When Trey lay content with milk dribbling from the
corner of his mouth, Julia pushed up to a sitting position
and searched for "red streak painful boob" on her laptop.
Dr. Google, beloved by patients and hated by actual
physicians worldwide, diagnosed herself with *mastitis*,
an infected milk duct. How come no one told her such a
thing existed? She'd heard of an infected tooth but an
infected milk duct? Would the fun never end?

She never called in sick to school or work, not
once—ever, something she prided herself on. But the day
had come with her fever up to one hundred and three and
pain up the wazoo. She left Carlton a voicemail with the
news.

The phone rang a minute later.

"Don't bother begging me to come in," she said.
"There's no way I can do it—not today."

"*¿Estás loca*? It's your mother calling."

"Oh, it's you. How are you, Mamá?"

"I had a dream last night. You were lying in a
hospital bed with four monkeys sitting on perches in
each corner of the room, watching you with glowing
green eyes—ready to attack." She sucked in her breath.
"Then—I burst into the room with a bow and arrow. I
was wearing the Sadie Hawkins dance dress from my
first year at Aguila High, which I sewed myself with
fabric I found at seventy-five percent off at Alma's
Sewing store—silvery pink with a sheer white scarf and
pearls, fake of course, but no one else knew that. I invited
Fausto Menendez to the dance that year—the most
handsome boy in my class. That was before I met your

father, of course. In the dream, my shoes—which I borrowed from…"

"*Aye*, Mamá, you have the strangest dreams," Julia interrupted, knowing her mother's dream could take half an hour to describe. "But I woke up feeling crappy this morning, so I suppose this dream was weirdly visionary. Body aches, a fever—Google says it's an infected milk duct."

"Milk duck? What kind of duck is *that*?"

"No." Julia started laughing, but it hurt, so she quickly stopped. "A milk duct—D.U.C.T.—in my mammary gland."

"*Aye*. Are you still feeding him from *there*? Yichhh. Try *carne asada* chopped up real fine. Or put it in the blender, although I admit that will look *most* unappetizing. I gave you refried beans at two months. Cook them with bacon; that'll be even better. Soak the beans overnight, then throw out the water in the morning to eliminate the—side effect."

"Farting?"

"*Aye*, no. Proper Mexican women don't F.A.R.T. Now—let's talk about the real reason for my call."

"Hell's bells. What's the real reason?"

"Money."

Julia rolled her eyes. "What about it?"

"Do you need any? I know how you two struggle, and now with little Raúl…"

"Trey?"

"Yes, yes, whatever. Have you started a college fund?"

"He's not even three months old."

"I figured as much. When I came into all that money from my Tío Ricardo, I invested it. I'm richer than the entire population of, oh, what's some small insignificant state? Delaware. Since you and Carlos don't have two nickels to rub together, I've earmarked some for my grandson's education—to Harvard or Yale or whatever Ivy League school he chooses. Of course, if I die before he turns eighteen, you'll get it all and do what you want. I'm a woman with a twenty-one-bedroom, twenty-four-bathroom mansion in Highland Park, a maid, a chef, a limo and personal driver, a hundred purses in every color, and twice as many pairs of shoes—expensive ones. I don't do cheap. *Mija*, I want to share my good fortune with you. I can buy you anything. Or send you a zillion dollars. Would you like that? I just sent you a new blender—the most expensive one on the market—to grind the *carne asada,* as I said. You're probably using a cheapy blender from some garage sale. You get what you pay for. Do you need a new car?"

"Thank you, Mamá, but we're doing all right." *But I might lose my job, and Charlie's teacher pay sucks the big one.* "Would you mind if we pick this conversation up later tonight or tomorrow? I need to call my doctor."

"How are you doing at losing the baby weight? Do you remember Valentina's daughter, Estella? She's back to a size four, and it's only been two months since she had her little Mateo. She's a runner, marathons and all that. Anyhooo, there's a new diet I read about where people eat like the Neanderthals. I doubted it at first, but apparently, it's…"

"Gotta run, Mother."

"Don't misinterpret me. I don't want you to be any more Neanderthal than the people there in the land of outdoorsy things already are. Isn't Washington State the official land of the Bigfoots? The women up there wear the ugliest sandals, and some don't even paint their toenails. They probably have hairy feet."

"Mother!"

"Tell Carlos to keep a golf club by the bed and watch for green-eyed gargoyles—doesn't he have green eyes himself? Hah. Maybe he's the gargoyle. And check into the Neanderthal diet. I'm sure you can find it on the computer."

"Thanks for calling. I love you." Julia waited, in the slight chance her mother might say, I love you back, but she didn't. Paloma never did believe in that lovey-dovey stuff. As much as Julia wanted 'I love yous' and full embraces as a kid, she never got more than awkward side hugs.

An hour later, despite having no appetite, she scarfed a Neanderthal favorite, a triple-decker peanut butter and apricot jam sandwich. She understood well the mixed messages her brain manufactured. Make Mamá proud and make her pay.

****

The room looked clean except for the magazine rack hanging on the wall with home decorating, parenting, and fashion magazines—wrinkled, ripped, and dog-eared. Julia glanced at them, imagining billions of nefarious germs from, eeewww—sick people. Tacked to the ceiling above the exam table, an image of a poppy field served as a distraction for every restless woman with a speculum in her cervix.

"Ya look like crap," Dr. Folger said in her Kentucky drawl. "Are ya getting any decent sleep? From the look-a-ya, I think not. Ya gotta stop pickin' that baby up every time ya hear him squeak in the middle of the night. It's not sustainable, hon."

"I sleep in spurts. And when I do *sleep*," Julia said, using quote fingers, "I'm half awake, waiting for him to wake up again."

It took all of three minutes into her appointment for her hurt, confusion, and guilt to tumble out in a mess of tears and confessions.

"I'm ashamed to admit it, but I wish I never had him." She looked around the six-by-six-foot room. "Shouldn't a lightning bolt come from the heavens to strike me down about now? I'm not meant for motherhood. I want to go shopping. I want to go to Ashland for the Shakespeare Festival and climb Mount Rainier on a clear sunny day. Not that I would ever climb Mount Rainier, mind you, but you get the point. I want to crochet a blanket with no interruptions. I want to try out for a musical at The Cascade City Players. I *can* sing, you know, and I've been called a drama queen more than a few times." She bit her lower lip and squeezed her eyes shut. "My shoulders stink like vomit, which I can smell whenever I turn my head. It's my *own* curdled milk which makes it even grosser."

"Girl, ya may feel alone in thee-iss, but yer not. I promise. Sumpin' like one in ten new moms git post-partum depression. It's caused by wackadoodle hormones, an' you aren't doin' anythin' wrong. Ya hear me? This is quite normal, and it'll pass."

Julia wiped her dripping nose with a burp cloth she pulled out of the baby bag.

Dr. Folger rubbed little circles on Julia's back. "Yer gonna be juss fine, ma dear."

Ten more minutes of spilling her guts and prescriptions for an antibiotic and an increased dosage of her antidepressant later, Julia hoisted Trey into the backseat, fastened him in, and checked her phone.

A text from Carlton arrived while she was talking to Dr. Folger about her sorry-ass life.

—Reminder. Pool w the big dogs tomorrow at Killians. Six p.m. drinks. Don't flake out.—

****

January 20, 2017
The Cascade City Chronicle

"Skateboarders and Dog Walkers Collide Around Popular Lake Chickadee"

Julia sat at her work desk wiping her ergonomic keyboard with a cotton swab soaked in alcohol, set as a recurring appointment on her calendar every Friday at eight a.m.

"There's got to be a way to save this place," she said to her laptop. She typed, "demise of local newspapers." Many articles spelled out the problem, including a report on the new operating model at *The Fort Worth Free Press*. She liked the idea. Would there be a way to pull it off in Cascade City? Had the Kellers already considered it?

Her phone rang.

"Hey," Jerry whispered. "Can you talk?"

"What's up?"

"Dirt on Booth."

"Where are you?" She wiped her glass-covered desk with an antibacterial wipe and rubbed it dry with a paper towel.

"In my car across the street."

"Then why are you whispering?"

"I don't know."

"I'll be right out."

Julia went through the employee turnstile. Her curly

hair frizzed into the shape of a Christmas tree when it hit the misty-moisty air.

Jerry sat in his red 1967 Mustang with thick white stripes across the hood and roof of the car. Hardly inconspicuous. He reached over and unlocked the door.

"Whatcha got?" Julia asked.

"This is getting juicy," he said, wide-eyed and giddy. "I interviewed the housekeeper at another rich guy's house—the one next to Booth's. She's worked there for twenty-four years. The name's, uh…" He paused to look at his reporter's notebook. "Lucia. According to her, a Hispanic woman showed up at Booth's house in 1997 when his wife, Dorthea, was dying of brain cancer. She figured the woman was a hospice nurse or something, but she never left, even after Dorthea died. Been there ever since."

"That must be Carmen's mother."

"Exactly. Lucia used to see the woman picking up the mail at the end of the driveway. They'd speak Spanish to each other—just small talk—until Lucia asked the woman, *Joanne*"—Jerry scrunched his lips to the side and shook his head—"about the bruises on her face."

"And?"

"*Joanne*, a fake name for sure, clammed up, and that was the last time Lucia saw her outside. Booth installed a mail slot in the door." His face lit up. "This could be big, Julia. Our Hollywood stud, albeit an antique stud, is controlling this Joanne lady's life and maybe beating her."

"But we don't have anything concrete—just a bunch of random pieces and gossip. How do we know the bruises Lucia saw didn't happen from a fall or something?"

"The job of an investigative reporter is to find as many pieces as possible and put them together. Get this. There is no government record of Joanne Cooper in Cascade City if her last name's the same as Carmen's. And here's the biggest shocker. There's no birth record for Carmen. She told you she was born here, right? I looked up the social security number she put on her application. It belongs to Ruth Anne Bolton, who died in 1995 at age eighty-seven in Littleton, Colorado."

Goose bumps sprung up on Julia's arms. "Are you serious?"

Jerry handed Julia a small spiral-bound pad emblazoned: Reporter's Notebook. "You're an undercover reporter now. You can try typing things into the notes app on your phone, but my fat thumbs are much less efficient than a pen and, in your case, a pencil sharp enough to pierce somebody's ear. Your assignment is to get Carmen to talk—she's our best source."

"And Ana at Mama Mendoza's. Booth and some senator from Florida eat there every Friday, and I think Ana knows more than she's letting on."

"Emerson Mathis? That guy's a bum. Figures he and Booth are friends. Go get 'em, tiger." Jerry put his hands up like claws.

"Easy there, kitty. I'm holding on to my sanity by a thread as it is."

"Breaktime's over." He held up a pretend microphone. "I'm off to review *Frank and Stein*. College freshmen Frank and Stein party, smoke reefer, drink beer shotgun-style, and compete for bragging rights with busty professor Alura Fawx, who may or may not be the serial killer New York City police want to nail."

Julia busted out laughing. "You made that up."

"Hell, no. Being a movie critic's not all it's cracked up to be. People think it's all fun and games, but I have to watch plenty of shitty movies and eat bad food."

"Yeah, tough life, huh, Jer? Let's go kick some Booth butt."

Chapter Thirteen

January 20, 2017— continued

Although Julia preferred to avoid "networking" and other pretentious bullshit, she could schmooze with the best of them when required. So she put a look-how-sociable-I-am smile on her face and prepared to rub elbows with some of the newspaper's decision-makers, or at the very least, people with more influence, pay, and testicles than she did. *The Chronicle's* eight vice presidents: circulation-Tim, newsroom-David, editorial-Alan, production-Louis, finance-Ed, information technology-Ruben, web content-Jacob, advertising-Maurice; sixteen white guy testicles in all; or if the rumors were correct, fifteen. Louis, Jerry once told her, may have suffered a tragic nut-imploding accident as a high school baseball pitcher.

Killian's Billiard Club fit the description of a "dive bar" perfectly with its black and gold-marbled fuzzy wallpaper, yellowish "mood lighting," a green and blue lava lamp by the cash register, and musty cigarette smell from back when it was still okay to smoke indoors.

"I safe mah faverit call girl—a ssseat," Carlton said, tapping the barstool beside him.

The bartender turned from where he stood, mixing a drink. "You a call girl, huh?" He looked Julia over slowly. "I got customers who'd love a tall, dark drink-a-water like yourself." He ran his tongue over his top lip. "You got a business card, honey? Or a phone number I can write on this here napkin?"

"Screw you and the horse you rode in on. I'm not *that* kind of call girl," Julia snapped.

The bartender stuck a toothpick in his mouth and sucked on it. "Suit yourself."

"Sssit down," Carlton instructed, smoothing back the thinning strands of hair on the sides of his head.

Julia removed her gloves and hung her jacket on a coatrack at the end of the bar. "What the hell was that? You embarrassed me." She looked around the place. "Where's everyone else? Is *he* from *The Chronicle*?" She motioned toward a man with thick black-rimmed glasses and short dark hair, two barstools over. "He looks familiar."

Carlton swiveled around to check the guy out. "My…be from the pressss…room er somethin'. Or a janitor? How should I know?"

"Didn't you say to be here at six o'clock?" She paused to look at her watch. "It's six thirty. Where are the other senior managers?"

"Other managersss? Ohhh, right. Mitchell's ole-lady wooden let 'im come."

He's piss-in-his-pants drunk. "What about everybody else? You tricked me."

"Albert's workin' late, an' Doug's a no-show. I spose iss juss you an' I, my spicy en-chill-aw-duh." His cigarette-stained teeth glistened under the lights when he smiled.

"It's 'me' not 'I,' and I can explain why that is to you another time because your seventh-grade English teacher obviously didn't do the job. Can we talk about the call center? You may not care, but I promised our employees that I'd fight for them—and I've been racking my brain. Do you know about *The Forth Worth Free Press*? Their business model could work if we found…"

"Whoa, whoa, whoa. Slow down der, pardner. Lemme gitcha a drink. What'll ya haff? Somethin' froooty? Or a mar-guh-ree-tuh? I bet they got tequila with the worrmmm in it. Your people like the worrmmm, dohn day? Hey. I said a Messican word. *Donde* means *where*."

Julia signaled the bartender. "Cola with lime?"

"You bet, 'not that kind of call girl,' " he replied.

Carlton pouted. "Hell, I thaw we my haff us some fun duhnight. You wahn haff some fffun?"

"You'd catch on fire if I lit a match right now. How much have you had of that stuff?"

"Number four right there," the bartender chimed in.

"Is anyone talking to you?" Julia barked.

The bartender crossed his arms. "Suit yourself."

Carlton took another swig of his whatever-on-the-rocks, stood up, and leaned into the bar with one elbow to hold himself up. A bit of skin and gray hair poked through his strained shirt buttons.

"Ya see, me an' Bessie's loss that lovin' feelin', an' I wanchooo ta hepp me fine it again."

The pulsing in Julia's temples turned to thrashing. "Ewwww, Carlton—are you saying what I think you're saying?"

"Mah doctor toll me I'm missin' vitamin U." He planted one hand firmly on her ass. "If you dohn wahn *do it*, you can juss suck my…"

Julia slapped his hand away. "What the? Don't you

ever touch me again. All this time, I've told myself you're nothing but a harmless old man *and* my boss, so I've put up with you. But you're—you're—a self-absorbed—sexist—prick. And dumb as a rock to boot."

"Did you say prick? Now we're talkin'." Carlton bobbed his head. "Pleeess? You wahn…mah job? I'm not askin' mush. We ken make it a quickie."

"I should've turned you in a long time ago." Julia grabbed her purse and coat and tromped toward the exit.

The man with the thick black glasses gawked at them unabashedly.

"Ya sure ya wanna walk out that door now? You wahn mah job er not, my li'l call girl?" Carlton yelled across the room.

Julia threw the door open and hurried to her car. No one walked the street, no car passed, and no human-made sound came from anywhere. Much of Cascade City's downtown core, including the two largest assisted living centers, shut their doors at six p.m. The shops closed, and residents turned in early to watch the news, gameshows, or reruns of the LoveLine channel's lineup of mushy Christmas movies. Few tourists visited in the winter when the clouds persistently tinkled on everything.

She drove to Seattle on the perpetually gridlocked I-5 freeway, parked near The Pike Place Market, and looked over a railing to the waterfront below. Lights glimmered across the waters of Puget Sound. The giant Ferris wheel illuminated in Seattle Seahawks blue and green turned on Elliott Bay. A cruise ship floated, like a moving city, toward Pier Sixty-Six.

She didn't like what she'd become: an oh-woe-is-me woman—exhausted, anxious, petulant, and waiting to feel normal again. A woman who let her prick boss get away with harassment. But what if "normal" never came back? What if she had to make peace with a new normal?

She thought of her mother—before the inheritance. Paloma worked full-time in the home appliances department of a now bankrupt and belly-up retailer. She kept the house clean enough to eat off the floor, tended to her father's every need, even when his health declined, knitted blankets for residents at the senior center, and made over fifty dozen tamales to give away at church each Christmas. And a thousand other things. *Shit happens when moms take charge.* She brought her clasped hands to her forehead, closed her eyes, and summoned the Wonderella she wanted to be.

Carlton's going to pay.
I'm going to get his job.
I'm going to save the world.
Or at least the call center.
And maybe the paper?
And Carmen. I'm going to save Carmen.
What's the deal with Carmen, anyway?
And make Charlie happy again.
And lose twenty pounds.
What did Neanderthals eat?
Triceratops?
Because they don't sell those around here.
I'll lose twenty pounds another time.
Another decade.
Maybe never.
But still, it could happen.
Anything can happen.
Shit happens when moms take charge.
Wonderella!
Yeah, that's me.

I should come up with a cool superhero outfit that covers up belly flub and back fat.

The increase in her antidepressant dosage led to the sudden uptick in hope and empowerment. Not her mother's tip about the Neanderthal diet. That did not help. Neither did Carlton's request for a blow job.

****

Trey and Charlie lay sleeping on the sofa, chest to chest. Baby bottles and beer bottles sat empty on the coffee table.

Julia carried Trey into his room. His curved eyelashes fanned out, and his full lips came together in the shape of a heart. Could he get any cuter? She transferred him from her arms to the crib mattress without waking him up. Thanks to the Big Guy Upstairs for that little miracle. Not that she believed in the Big Guy Upstairs, but from time to time, she thanked him—just in case.

She tiptoed into the bathroom and sat on the bed when Charlie appeared in the doorway.

"Hi, babe. You're home late. How did everything go?" he mumbled, mid-yawn.

"You wouldn't believe the day I've had."

"You wanna talk about it?"

"You're half asleep. We can talk about it in the morning."

"I gotta go in early, remember?" He pulled off his sweatshirt and pants and tossed them on the wooden chair by the bedroom window. "Lesson planning for the kiddos. With all the master's homework, I'm constantly behind on lesson planning."

"How was Trey tonight?"

"He laughed for the first time, hon—a real laugh. I

played peek-a-boo with him, and it was the sweetest thing I ever heard." Charlie undressed, climbed in bed, turned over, and that was it—deep breathing, then a light rumbly snore.

How many other things will I miss while I'm at work? Sitting up? Crawling? Walking? First word? Julia shuffled to the kitchen and dove into a carton of salted caramel ice cream. Wonderella needed a boost of the carbohydrate variety.

Chapter Fourteen

January 23, 2017
The Cascade City Chronicle

"Retired Senator Mathis Bemoans State's 'Socialist Tendencies' "

Carmen's alarm went off at five thirty a.m. She rubbed the sleep out of her eyes, dressed, and tiptoed downstairs. Like every year, on January 23rd, it would be a day of walking on eggshells. She expected a miserable day.

She opened the late nineteenth-century French buffet and chose a cup from Dorthea's fine china. She filled it with cognac and a splash of coffee, and set it on a tray with a napkin and blueberry muffin. She walked up the stairs, taking care not to spill, but her flip-flop caught the edge of the final step. The tray flew as if in slow motion. The panic set in as she watched.

Papa Percy appeared in his bedroom doorway. "You, clumsy fool. Of *all* days to do something so fucking stupid."

She could smell the alcohol on his breath from ten feet away. "I'm sorry, Papa. I'll be right back with more cognac and another muffin." She flew down the stairs.

Booth came after her.

****

She heard the swish-swish of Mami's slippers against the white marble tile floor. "Mami! Stay out!" she screamed.

Consuelo entered the kitchen, looking down as she fiddled with the zipper on her robe. "Wha' joo mean 'Don't come…' " She lifted her head, and the color drained from her face. "Señor, wha' joo doing?"

Carmen stood at the counter near the coffee pot. Booth held his gold-handled revolver against her temple. One of Dorthea's watercolor sunrise paintings hung on the wall behind him. A bird with an upturned wing flew across a sunrise atop layers of gray-green hills.

Consuelo dropped to her knees. "Pleesss, pleesss, no. Tell me wha' joo wahn. I do anyting joo wahn." She clutched the cross around her neck.

Booth sneered. "You gave birth to this worthless excuse for a human being; that was enough. She's been watching me and writing in her notebook. I've seen her do it. And who is she talking to about me? A professor? A school counselor? She's against me. She's going to turn me in. But I've done nothing wrong. She'll lie through her teeth about me and get away with it." His bloodshot eyes stayed on Carmen the entire time. His grip on the revolver remained steady.

"Puneesh me," Consuelo sobbed. "Joo dohn wahn to hurt her. She your…" She glanced at Carmen. "She weel do better—I prromees. Iss my fault, *Señor*."

Booth's eyes became wet and glossy. "Today is Dorthea's birthday," he said and wiped a tear. "I thought you'd bring me comfort. But you've never measured up—not even close."

Consuelo held up both hands. "Jess, jess, I know. I prepare Dorthea's favorite brekfass, okay? I make stuff

French toas' weeth…"

"I'm tired," Booth said, lowering the gun. "So, so tired."

Carmen bolted, grabbing her backpack on the way out. She looked over her shoulder. Mami stood in the open doorway, clinging to Papa Percy's arm—the one with the gun pointed at her. She ran three blocks down a major thoroughfare, past two gas stations, a pizza joint, a German auto-body shop, and a medical building. She returned to the backroads, careful not to stay on any one street too long. She watched for Papa Percy's black four-door sedan with tinted windows as she approached *The Chronicle*.

****

Kelvin arrived to work at half past six, his usual start time. He glanced at the phone system monitor—a nice, slow morning.

"Kelvin? Can you take a customer call for me?" Sistine asked.

"Hey, Sistine," Kelvin replied. "What's goin' on?"

"Lola's calling again. I'm good with customers; you know that. But she takes it too far. Too far, I tell you." She patted her ears. "She makes my ears hurt."

"Okay, okay. For you, Sistine, I'll talk to Miss Lola." He followed her back to her workstation.

Sistine, wearing a knee-high black and gray plaid pleated skirt, a gray puffy-sleeved button-up blouse with pearl buttons, ruffled ankle socks and shiny-red flats, handed Kelvin her headset.

"Good mornin', Miss Lola," Kelvin said.

"Don't choo good mornin' me," Lola, one of the call center regulars, shouted.

"You don't sound too happy, Miss Lola."

"I'm sittin' here naked as a jaybird."

"Is that right? This is Kelvin. What can I do for ya?"

"I'm cuttin' my toenails, goddamnit. An I ain't got no garbage can to put 'em in. The nincompoop at the front desk said he didn't have no other one to bring me. I think he got hemorrhoids in his mouth; that's what I think."

"Where are ya, Miss Lola?"

"At the motel on Crow Road, ya bloviated bovine."

"Have ya thought about dumpin' your toenails in the toilet, Miss Lola? Just sweep 'em up with your hand. That could work."

"Oh," Lola said and hung up.

"Gotta love Miss Lola," Kelvin told Sistine as he returned her headset. "Never a dull day around here. That's what I love about it."

"I don't like Miss Lola, and you know it. She gets me all excited—and not in a good way."

"It's too easy to do, Sistine, you must admit."

"I'll do no such thing." Sistine sat back down, smoothed her skirt, and pushed a blinking light on her phone set. "*Cascade City Chronicle*, this is Sistine. May I help you?"

Kelvin left to get coffee at the vending machine. Halfway there, he stopped mid-step and frowned. Carmen stood by the door to the employee entrance dressed in gray sweats, a T-shirt, and house slippers. Her backpack hung from one hand.

****

Kelvin lived in the Waterside Apartments, a peculiar name because no natural body of water existed within a ten-mile radius, except for the potholes after a good rain. Houses with neglected cars, peeling paint, and overgrown weeds, graffiti-splashed apartment buildings, a dilapidated Buzzy's Dollar Mart, a shuttered Paco's Tacos with plywood over the windows, and a shabby community center gave the neighborhood its reputation as the "iffy part of town." The well-to-do Cascade City residents avoided it. The senior crowd was afraid of it. Not the spot tourists frequented either, and one the city officials pretended didn't exist.

He pulled into a numbered parking spot, and they walked up three flights of steps.

"It's not much, but it's home," he said to Carmen, scrambling to grab dirty dishes off a metal TV tray with an orange and yellow daisies design he got for free at a garage sale. "I wasn't expectin' company, or I woulda cleaned up."

The two-bedroom, one-bath apartment had a sofa, a card table with two white fold-up plastic chairs, a giant TV, a videogame console, another TV tray with a record player on top, and two knee-high stacks of old-school records on the floor: Marvin Gaye, Al Green, Aretha, Ray Charles, The Commodores, and Barry White.

"I don't mind it," Carmen said. "My *life's* a mess. I'm just thankful you said 'yes,' and that you could get away from work."

"I left Monty in charge. He'll be fine if he doesn't light a joint at the front desk. I'm still surprised as heck about your whole situation, though. What kinda father threatens to kill his daughter?"

"He's not my father."

"But you called him 'Papa Percy.' "

"It's complicated."

Kelvin showed her to the sofa, but she stopped at the window and peered through the blinds to the street below.

"And *how* long ya been livin' with this fella?"

"I was born in his house," she said before sitting down. "And there are no records of it. No birth certificate. I've got a social security number, but it's fake. He must have bought it from somebody. Please don't tell anyone."

"Giirrl, it *does* sound complicated. I have a zillion questions, but I won't pry for now. Okay if I sit with you?"

Carmen nodded. "I'll only stay until I can find a place for my mother and me—a shelter or something. I'll never forgive myself if he hurts her. Who knows what he'll do if I'm not there."

"Shouldn't we call the police?"

"I would have called them a long time ago if it was that simple. Trust me. They'd do more harm than good."

"I reckon I can understand that. Do ya know how many times I been pulled over in this town for drivin' while black? Or walkin' while black? Or shoppin' while black? Or standin' still while black? Wasn't much better in Oklahoma neither, and there were lots more of us black folk there."

With the long gold sofa cushion sagging in the middle, Carmen could feel his radiating warmth, and it felt good—a man sitting next to her—one who could block a slap to the face, a shove to the back, or a gun to the temple. She wiped a tear with her forearm.

Kelvin patted her back gently. "Okay, c'mon then. Let's getcha settled in your room, aka my office. We don't have to solve the problems right now, do we?" He held out his hand and helped her up.

The spare bedroom-slash-office wasn't much larger

than the supply room at work, and it suited Carmen just fine. She looked around in awe.

"What?" Kelvin asked.

"It's got a futon, a desk, a lamp, and a chair."

Kelvin arched an eyebrow. "Yes, ma'am. Is that alright with you?"

"Yes, of course. All I have is a lamp in my bedroom at home." She cleared her throat. "I mean, Papa Percy's house. It was never my home." She plopped her backpack on the futon and pulled out her diary. "I'm using this to build up my courage."

"Courage for what?"

"To stop being afraid. To *do* something." Carmen held out the diary. "This will help you understand why I had to run away."

"A gun to your head was plenty enough reason, don't ya think?"

"Yeah, but it's more than that. For all your kindness, you deserve to know. I trust you, Kelvin. I'm not sure why because we haven't known each other that long, but I do."

Chapter Fifteen

January 24, 2017
The Cascade City Chronicle

"St Luke's Seeks Funds for New Kindergarten-Twelve School"

Julia heard the all too familiar sounds. Her son didn't know if he wanted to babble or bawl. She rolled over to look at the clock—three forty a.m. Shit. Crap. Doodoo. *Please, God. Make him sleep some more.*

The flat-out bawling ensued a minute later.

Charlie, as usual, slept through Trey's middle-of-the-night shenanigans.

Men. They can hear a beer can open at the next-door neighbor's barbecue but not a baby screaming across the hall.

She shuffled to Trey's room, fed him, changed his diaper, and arranged him on her thighs, face-up, his head near her knees. She grabbed his feet and pushed his legs back and forth in a cycling motion, which, Dr. Google said, would help him pass gas.

"In what other scenario would I encourage someone to fart in my direction?" she asked him. Of course, he obliged and farted.

The doorbell rang three times in rapid succession.

"Who in the hell is that?" She held Trey close and

ran into the bedroom. "Charlie!" She pushed on his shoulder. "There's someone at the door."

Charlie rolled from his side to his back and rubbed his eyes. "What?"

"There's someone at the door. Go answer it. It could be someone in trouble. Or a guy with a butcher knife." She flipped on the light.

"Okay, okay. Let me pull on my robe. What time is it? Jesus. It's four o'clock in the morning."

The doorbell rang again.

"Coming!" Charlie hopped around, trying to step into his slippers.

"Really? You need your slippers to answer the door?"

"The floor's cold." Charlie trotted to the front entry and opened the door.

Paloma left her suitcases on the front porch, strode past Charlie, and took Trey from Julia's arms. "Hola! Hola! This must be my *gorgeous* grandson. There, there, my *Raulito*," Paloma soothed. "Shhh…shhh, it's going to be all right. Your *abuelita* is here to take care of you. Has your mother been feeding you that *carne asada* we discussed? Are you hungry, my Raulito? Shall I make you some *frijoles*?"

Julia and Charlie stared at each other and then at Paloma. Charlie's mouth hung so far open you could have shoved in a tennis ball.

"Mamá? What on earth are you doing here?" Julia croaked.

Paloma wore navy slacks with perfectly ironed pleats, a cream cashmere sweater, navy high-heel sandals, a sapphire necklace, and diamond drop earrings with gems the size of grapes. Her nails sported cabernet-red polish. "Where are your manners, Julia? Invite me to sit down. I'm holding my grandson, for goodness sake."

"I'm sorry, Paloma. Please, sit," Charlie said. "I'll get your suitcases and put them—put them…" He looked at Julia, shook his head, and lifted his shoulders. "Where should I put them?"

"Mamá, we only have two bedrooms, and one is the baby's room," Julia explained.

"Doesn't he have a bassinet?" Paloma handed Julia her navy designer purse. "You can move him into your room. It's only for one night, *Mija*. I'm checking into a bed and breakfast on the beach tomorrow. Juanita, my housemaid, checked reviews on the computer. She picked a five-star place, the best breakfast in town, warm chocolate chip cookies in the afternoon, and a lovely little gift shop. Apparently, they sell coffee beans. Everywhere, coffee. You must be the sleepiest people in the nation. And the most hyperactive. You know, you don't have any *real* hotels in this tiny town in the toolies, not even a Hilton. I suppose that's what you get when you live in the sticks with the Bigfoots." Paloma glanced around the room. "Hmph. I'll sit in the rocking chair. Your sofa appears as if it comes from a checkered past."

Sitting in the chair with her tiny little thighs pressed together, Paloma brought Trey to within an inch of her face. Julia never liked sitting that way—too much work and entirely impractical for any woman with a body mass index more than the legal drinking age.

"*Como estás, mi corazón*?" Paloma cooed. "Are you tired? Don't you worry. I'll rock you right to sleep. I have a way with babies. Unless you're hungry. I can make you some chocolate chip cookies without Mexican vanilla because they don't sell it here." She threw Julia a sideways glance.

"Mother, you still haven't explained why you're here. You didn't tell us you were coming." Julia felt more exasperated with each passing second. Charlie stood still, his expression a mix of WTF and about-to-puke.

"*Aye*. Do I need an invitation to see my grandson? My one and only? Unless you plan to give me a second one soon? A girl, perhaps? I have lots of jewelry to hand down. Very expensive jewelry, I might add. A dark-haired girl with Carlos' green eyes and a tiny frame would be very nice."

"I can barely handle the crybaby, I mean 'the kid' I have."

"*Mija*, get me a cola, in a glass with plenty of ice. I came to see my grandson. If I'd waited until you invited me, he'd be married with children of his own. Besides, ever since that dream about the gargoyles, I haven't been able to rest peacefully."

"I'll get the soda," Charlie offered. He returned with an open can and handed it to Paloma. "Gargoyles?" he asked.

"Thank you, Carlos, but I *said*, 'in a glass, with lots of ice.' "

"Oops," Charlie replied. "It's hard to follow directions at four a.m. when someone shows up at your door unannounced."

"You didn't tell him about my dream, *Mija*? You may laugh about my dreams, but those gargoyles seemed real to me."

"Look, Mother—let's get you settled," Julia said. "You're going to have to sleep on the sofa with the checkered past."

"*Aye*, no. I won't sleep on that thing. I'll stay up with Raulito. Show me where you keep the bottles and formula. I'll take over."

"I might as well stay up," Charlie said, holding the glass of soda. "I've got to go in soon anyway."

"Mother, I'm going back to bed," Julia announced. "Bring the baby to me if he starts to fuss. He'll be hungry soon."

"No, no—none of *that* while I'm here. Please tell me you don't do the natural mother thing in *public*. You don't live in a commune."

"What are you talking about?"

"Oh, God. I hope I didn't give you any ideas. You hear that, Carlos? You are not allowed to move my daughter and grandson to a commune. I heard the northwest's littered with them." Paloma stood up and held Trey over her shoulder. "I'll find the bottles myself."

Julia crawled into bed. Charlie came in after his shower dressed in khakis, a deep green button-up shirt, and brown slip-on shoes.

"Your mother's a trip. I hope you don't throttle her when I'm not around."

"How about when you *are* around?"

Chapter Sixteen

January 24, 2017—continued

Julia took Trey to the daycare, ignoring her mother's pleas to leave him with her. She agreed to let Paloma pick him up at daycare at two o'clock, after his second nap. Despite Paloma having the maternal warmth of a hockey rink, Julia felt comfortable leaving her two-and-a-half-month-old with her. *It's temporary*, she reasoned.

****

She walked through *The Chronicle* lobby, past the payroll window, the finance department, and the mailroom, where her employee, Monty, once photocopied fifteen pages of his bare butt during the night shift, handwrote "Good Moonin" on each page, and laid them on call center desks.

"It would have been more efficient to write 'Good Moonin' on the first one and *then* photocopy it," she told him before handing him his written warning. He seemed genuinely surprised that using company equipment for such a purpose broke a policy or two. "Are you kiddin' me, man? I thought it was funny," he said.

Afterward, Julia wrote a thank you note to the facilities lady who had the unfortunate job of sanitizing the copy machine glass.

A familiar symphony of voices filled the room—

taking orders, canceling subscriptions, entering vacation holds, apologizing for missed deliveries and the like. She stepped into her cubicle, jumped back, and smacked her chest in surprise. "You scared me."

"Why ya so scared? Never seen a big black dude sittin' in your chair?"

"Knock it off, you—you—big black dude," she said, grinning. "I wasn't expecting *anyone* there."

"I need to talk to ya about somethin'," Kelvin replied, his big smile suddenly absent.

"What's up?" She frowned. "Is something wrong?"

Kelvin looked over his shoulder. "Can we go somewhere more private?"

"How about the cafeteria? We can find a quiet table near the back."

Kelvin squeezed his hands together. "Somebody might hear us there."

"All right, let's go find an empty office. Someone's bound to be on vacation."

They wandered until they found one in the home delivery department. Kelvin closed the door.

"Don't tell me you're leaving us for Oklahoma," Julia said.

"No, it's not that at all. It's Carmen."

The hairs on Julia's arms stood up.

Kelvin ran his hand across the top of his head. "Some old guy's been keepin' her locked up. And her momma along with her."

"What do you mean 'keeping her locked up?' She goes to school and work." Her mind whirled like a salad spinner as she struggled to make sense of it.

"She goes to school, but that's it. He doesn't know she works here. He thinks she's at the college library when she's at *The Chronicle*."

"And she told you this?"

"That's just it. She's stayin' at my place. I'm not gonna get in trouble, am I? Me bein' the lead and all? It's nothin' romantic. I'm just helpin' her as a friend. She ran away and didn't have anywhere else to go."

"No, no, don't worry about that." Julia leaned forward and looked squarely into his eyes. "Is she in danger? Be straight with me."

"He threatened to shoot her yesterday mornin'," he continued. "I'm not exaggeratin'. Held the gun right to her head. He'd been drinkin' all night. Carmen ran off but had to leave her momma behind."

Julia put her hand over her mouth. "Oh, dear Lord. You mean Percy Booth?"

"How'd you know?"

"I had a scary encounter with him on Carmen's first day when she didn't show up for her shift. Remember that?"

He frowned. "Yes, I do. I thought ya said you'd leave the situation alone."

"That's what *you* said. Anyway, I drove to Carmen's house to check on her. Ole Percy came outside and showed me his fancy gun up close and personal. The guy's a psycho. I've been worried about Carmen ever since but didn't have anything concrete to go on."

"Carmen let me read her diary from when she was a kid. She's been scared of him forever, though it sounds like he's been gettin' meaner. And drunker."

Julia tapped her fingertips on her forehead. "If Booth threatened to kill her, we've got to report it to the cops, Kelvin. Especially if her mother's still in the house."

He shook his head. "She'll run if we get them involved—she made that real clear. She and her momma don't have the right papers to be here. They'll get deported."

"Fuckity fuck. Immigrants are being held in cages on the border as we speak. But not the Canadian border, mind you. Just the border where brown people fleeing poverty and violence cross." She rested her elbow on the table, chin in hand. "I can understand why Carmen would be terrified. The police would have to get immigration authorities involved, and the police in Cascade City aren't used to dealing with much more than jaywalking tourists and the occasional car prowl. Who knows what they'd do."

Kelvin nodded in agreement. "And to make matters worse, somebody in Mexico wants Consuelo dead. They can never go back."

"Oh geez, Kel. Will Carmen be at work tomorrow?"

"She didn't say she *wasn't* comin', but she may be afraid to leave my apartment 'cause Booth could be lookin' for her or callin' the bad dudes in Mexico. He threatens Carmen and her momma with that all the time."

"Ask her to stop by when she gets here. I can't help her if she doesn't talk to me."

"She's gonna be very unhappy with me for tellin' ya. But I didn't know what else to do. She doesn't have family around or a friend in the world. Isn't that sad? I'm it, I guess."

Julia tilted her head and touched his shoulder. "We'll help her together, okay? Booth is gonna get what he deserves."

****

Jerry and Julia went out for drinks for the first time

in 2012. Three Midori martinis and a pear-gorgonzola crostini later, and he started yakity-yakking his guts up. They closed the place down at two o'clock in the morning when the bartender kicked them out.

Having been the subject of relentless teasing for most of his childhood, Gerald Pitstik legally changed his name to Jeremiah Dean—after James Dean, the tragically hot movie star and cultural icon of teenage angst and rebellion, long since gone. Since dopes near and far couldn't spell "Jeremiah," he went by "Jerry" to eliminate the headache.

It was bad enough to be the tender-hearted, height-challenged boy on the playground, but *Pitstik*? Pitstik most definitely had to go, Jerry told her. His parents tried shaming him into changing his mind about the last name with, "Honor your father and mother that it may go well with you and that you may live long in the land," but Jerry became Jeremiah Dean anyway. He knew he couldn't please his parents no matter what he did or how well he did it. He never told them outright he was gay, but the purple fingernails, lilting voice, and peach-colored satin jacket he bought with his allowance money on his twelfth birthday probably gave it away. Mom and Dad Pitstik tolerated Jerry from an early age, but dyeing his hair neon green was the final straw. After that, they fully supported, even encouraged, the name change.

The same day Jerry signed the papers at the municipal court, he gathered what he could carry and moved out. He slept on park benches and in rain-protected nooks of retail storefronts in Seattle's Capitol Hill neighborhood, where homosexuals and other gender nonconformists fit in. He still lived in an apartment on the corner of Twelfth Avenue and East Howe Street, overlooking Lake Union.

Thirty-one years passed, and not once did Jerry tell his parents where he was, and, as far as he could tell, they never tried to find him. He promised himself he'd make it big one day—and working at a smallish tourist town newspaper as the arts and entertainment critic wasn't cutting it. He needed something bigger, splashier, more *now*-are-you-proud-of-me? The Booth story could change everything, and Merle and Marie Pitstik would know about it. He drove by the family home occasionally and saw *The Chronicle* on the porch.

****

Jerry and Julia walked through the newsroom; Julia in stretchy black pants and a sensibly loose black Rayon blouse and Jerry in fuschia jeans, a starched white cotton shirt, a thick black belt and bedazzled white platform tennis shoes. His platinum hair, short on the sides, stood up spikey in the front.

Disheveled towers of paper covered every desk in the place. If the long overdue Cascadia earthquake hit, the floor would become an impenetrable sea of documents only Moses could part. Six reporters, a photojournalist, a news librarian, and a web designer sat typing, talking on the phone, or dozing off. Marv, the lone copyeditor, looked like he'd been there for decades, accumulating dust. Two fresh-eyed college interns stood in a corner, chattering over their morning lattes and high-protein egg bites. A line of ceiling-mounted TVs streamed news programs and the *Serenity Channel*, with nature scenes and calming computer graphics aimed at lowering stress, which no one watched.

They found an office behind the break room, closed the shades, and Jerry continued his search of public records on Percy Booth. Five minutes later, he turned his laptop toward Julia to show her something on hollywoodhounds.com.

"In 1971," it read, "Booth allegedly stole a Victorian-era horseshoe brooch with thirty-six emeralds from the set of *The Gunslinger*, where he met wife number four, Dorthea, who played Hattie, the saloon prostitute with one three-word line: 'Gimme another, Buddy.' Spectacle Studios confronted Booth with evidence from an eyewitness, Booth denied taking it, and the charge got dropped. The studio did its best to keep its accusation under wraps, and the brooch never materialized."

"It's interesting fodder," Julia said, "but it has nothing to do with Carmen."

Jerry flipped the pages in his reporter's notebook and glanced over what he'd written the day before: Dorthea's son: Stanford Simms, LA, phone number 213-555-0505

"Stanford, eh?" he said. "Maybe he can connect some dots."

Julia gave him a quizzical look.

"The stepson," he continued. "Let's see what he has to say." He punched the numbers into his cell phone and put it on speaker.

"Hello?" answered a woman.

"Stanford Simms, please."

"Of course. I'll transfer you now."

It rang twice before a man picked up. "Yes?"

"My name's Jeremiah Dean from *The Cascade City Chronicle* in Washington State. I want to talk to Stanford Simms about Percy Booth. Is this a good time?"

"What about him?" the man on the other end said.

"So, this *is* Stanford Simms?"

"Is Percy dead?"

Jerry cleared his throat. "Uh, no. He's not dead. He…"

"That's too bad."

Julia held her palms up in the WTF position.

"I said that he's *not* dead," Jerry repeated.

"And I said, 'That's too bad.' Look. I try not to think about that son of a bitch. What is it you want to know? I have about five minutes. I'm at work."

Jerry grabbed his pen.

"Can I confirm that you are Percy Booth's stepson? That he married your mother, Dorthea Simms, in 1975 when you were five?"

"Stop right there. Percy married my mother, and I lived with them in Hollywood and Cascade City, but I was *never* his stepson. He loved my mother; I'll give him that. But I was nothing more than baggage as far as he was concerned, and he treated me like dog shit. I haven't seen Percy since the day my mom died. I've got to go, Mr.—Bean, is it?"

"It's Dean, Jeremiah Dean. If you hate Booth as much as you say, I may have an opportunity you can't pass up."

Silence.

"Are you still there?" Jerry asked.

"Let me patch you through to my assistant, Stella. She can set up another time for you to tell me what this is all about."

As Stella's line rang, Jerry's face lit up. "This is happening," he said to Julia.

Jerry and Stella firmed up the details, and he drummed his feet against the floor in excitement.

Julia stood. "Time for a smoke break," she said. "Loading dock. I've got big news of my own. We're cookin' now. Wonderella and her sidekick Jerry."

"It's Almighty Jerry and his sidekick Wonderella."

Julia narrowed her eyes and stuck out her tongue. "Ladies first, remember?"

****

They stood behind an eighteen-wheeler full of five-hundred-pound newsprint rolls. Billows of breath swirled in the frigid winter cold as Julia told Jerry that Booth held a gun to Carmen's head and that Carmen was in hiding at Kelvin's apartment.

"You sure you're ready to handle what we're about to do?" Jerry asked Julia.

"And what is that exactly?"

"Take down a member of the Hollywood elite. Expose him for who he is and what he's done to those women. What a story it'll make." Jerry moved his open hand across an imaginary headline. "I'm thinking Pulitzer Prize."

"First things first, Jerry. Let's talk about getting the police involved."

"And blow our chance for the story of a lifetime? It'll hit the news way before we're ready. No fucking way. Let's get the facts together. We've got plenty of snooping around to do before we take that step, but we better get our shit together soon. Ask Carmen if she thinks her mother is in imminent danger. If so, we'll reassess."

"Okay." Julia looked at her wristwatch. "She'll be here in six hours." She stuffed her red, stiff hands into her pockets. "Did I tell you that my mother showed up at our door a few days ago?"

120

"Paloma? I *love* that woman."

Julia crossed her arms over her chest. "You've never met her."

"Dallas high society? Big hair? Designer clothes? Enough money to fill the Taj Mahal? What's not to love?"

"She and I couldn't be more different. You sure you can love us both?"

"A person can love chocolate *and* vanilla, right?"

"Yeah, but I'm the vanilla, and she's not chocolate. She's a banana split with gummy worms, sprinkles, and a cherry on top."

"Oh, come on. I'm not too fond of banana splits or gummy worms, and you should give yourself more credit. You're more like mocha almond fudge than vanilla. You'll have to introduce me to Paloma. We can compare purses. How long do you think she'll stay?"

"She hinted that it could be a while. I don't know if I can handle her and everything else I've got going on."

"Come on, Wonderella. You're a badass, and you can do anything you want."

"Yeah—I'm badass." Julia grabbed a section of hair and twirled a long curl around her finger. "Tell me again?"

"You're a badass."

"Damn straight. Either that or I've just got a bad ass."

"You need to love yourself for who you are, not who your mother wants you to be," Jerry replied. "And I think your ass is top rate."

"Thanks, Jer. My mother still looms large in my head, no matter how hard I try to forget the shit she pulled. There's a lot of history between us, most of it as pretty as a—a proboscis monkey—not that I've ever seen one in person, only on the nature shows."

"*What* kind of monkey?"

"The one with a giant dangling nut sack for a nose."

"What's so unattractive about a giant nut sack?"

"You're a sick fuck, Jerry."

****

"He's been so good—not a whimper out of him, and we've bonded already," Paloma gushed when Julia got home. "I wanted to take him shopping to replace the clothes you probably got for cheap at some poor people's store, but I was too worn out to manage it."

"Since when are you too tired to shop?" Julia asked. "I never thought the day would come."

"I called Juanita, my personal assistant, and told her to order him ten new outfits from Palmer's Department Store—they carry all the top brands. He'll be the sharpest dressed baby at the daycare."

"The clothes I put him in are just fine, but thanks anyway."

"I think I'll head back to the B&B now, *Mija*. I'm exhausted." Paloma stood, grimaced, and put her hand on her low back.

"Hmmm. Are you alright?"

"Old age, nothing more."

Chapter Seventeen

January 25, 2017
The Cascade City Chronicle

"Bingo Night at the Otter Club Moves to Thursdays"

Trey woke up three times, and Julia let him cry it out on the final go around—something she'd never done before. She could practically feel wrinkles setting in. *He can't be that hungry*, she reasoned. *Dr. Folger says I've been practically training him to wake up every two hours. He cries. I run in. He gets fed. Like Pavlov's dog. Smart kid. Or at least as smart as Pavlov's dog. Trey's okay. He's okay. He's okay.*

He screamed for sixteen heart-breaking minutes before he went back to sleep.

She tossed from side to side, trying to think of nothing.

Nothing, nothing, nothing.

Gah! My mother showed up at our door.

What is that all about?

Stop it, stupid brain. Think of nothing.

Nothing, nothing, nothing.

How can a person think of nothing? That's ridiculous.

Do I have ADHD?

I probably have ADHD.

I should call Dr. Folger about my ADHD.

Plus, I have a weird mole on my thigh. Will it sprout a hair?

Or hairs. A community of hairs.

Forget about the mole.

About Carmen and her mother…

Stop listening to Jerry and call the cops. It's too much responsibility.

If I call the cops, will some burly Homeland Security guy cart Carmen and her mom off in handcuffs?

What are the rules about this stuff?

Who do they deport, and who gets to stay?

What goes on in Booth's house?

I don't want to make the wrong decision.

And Carlton. That lowlife.

Can't avoid him forever.

I need to talk to Mei in HR. Time to rat on that revolting boss of mine.

Julia chewed her fingernails—a childhood habit she'd long since given up.

With everything I've got going on, I deserve a boatload of oatmeal with a shit-ton of butter and brown sugar. And half-n-half.

Stop thinking.

Nothing, nothing, nothing.

****

She smelled it the moment she opened his door. Trey pooped up his back, all over the crib sheet and down his legs. She put him on the changing table and opened his diaper.

"Oh, sweetie." An angry rash covered his butt, inside and out. "I'm so sorry, baby." She pulled off his pajama top, which smeared poop in his hair. "The one time I made you cry it out, and look what happened. If there's such a thing as mother's intuition, I don't have it."

She laid him in his plastic baby tub, set it inside the big tub, picked out the softest washcloth she could find, and started a stream of warm water. She sang "Itsy Bitsy Spider," and "You Are My Sunshine." Trey watched her intently and cooed like he wanted to sing, too. Until she tried to clean off his sensitive, bump-covered behind, at which time he scrunched his face and wailed.

Afterward, she ate oatmeal with a shit-ton of butter, brown sugar, and cream, then tried to force her ballooning butt and thighs into her stretchiest size-fourteen pants.

Nope.

She stomped to the garbage can in the side yard, threw the pants in, and kicked the can for good measure, but slipped on the wet gravel underneath, fell backward, and scraped the fleshy pads of both palms. She might have broken her tailbone if it hadn't been for that ballooning butt—an anatomical silver lining of sorts.

Before they left the house, she took her typed morning schedule off the refrigerator door and threw it in the recycle bin.

****

She walked into work late, wearing black maternity pants, the elastic front panel covered by a burgundy tunic. Her long curly hair, usually tied back, hung down her back. She brought her toothpaste and toothbrush from home to save time, hoping to steal away to the bathroom before talking to anyone.

Mei Tanaka emerged from behind the HR counter.

"Good morning, Julia. Haven't seen you in a while. Monty handing out any butt pics again?"

"Good morning, Mei. No butt pics today, but I need to talk to you," Julia replied, backing up a few steps to maintain a car-length distance. *How far does dragon breath travel?*

"Sure," Mei answered, looking at the calendar on her phone. "Looks like my nine thirty got canceled. Does that work for you?"

"Absolutely. See you then." Julia breathed into her cupped hand and made like a speed walker to the nearest bathroom, toothbrush ready.

****

Two steps into the call center, Wayne, a quiet older gentleman, his back the shape of Little Bo Peep's staff, approached. As a teen, he lost an index and middle finger in a tragic cheese-shredding machine accident at a pizzeria job. His typing skills sucked, and he took longer to get things done than other CSRs, but customers and Julia liked him. The year she knitted gloves as holiday gifts for her employees, she made an eight-fingered pair for Wayne, bringing him to tears. When her son was born and her spare time evaporated, she dropped knitting like a bad stitch. Occasionally, she picked up her knitting needles only to put them away again out of guilt for not doing something more essential like folding laundry, dusting, scrubbing a toilet bowl, or creating a checklist she'd fail to complete.

"Julia? I hate to trouble you," Wayne said.

"You're never any trouble, Wayne."

He pressed a curled knuckle over his lips.

"Is something wrong?"

"Sistine says I can't sit next to her. I'd find another

desk, but it's the only one available."

"What the heck? Did she say why?"

Wayne shifted his weight from foot to foot. "I think you should ask *her*."

Julia pulled her cafeteria card out of her wallet and handed it to him. "Go get yourself something downstairs. My treat."

"That's awfully generous." He took the card. "Sorry about the trouble."

"Bring me a cinnamon roll, will ya? It's part of my Neanderthal diet. See you in a few."

Julia weaved through the desks to get to Sistine. She was easy to spot in her white beret, red and navy plaid pants, navy sweater with kitty cat buttons up the front, and sparkly red shoes with a strap across the top—like the kind you click your heels in and make a wish to go home. A white daisy hairclip pinned back her flaming red hair to one side.

Sistine hit the "unavailable" button on her phone as Julia approached, crossed her legs, and rested her folded hands on her knee. "Good morning, Julia. Don't you look beautiful today," she said, smiling brightly.

"Good morning, Sistine. Thank you—as do you. Wayne says that you won't let him sit next to you," Julia replied, nodding to the empty desk on Sistine's left.

The smile disappeared from Sistine's face. "Is that a problem?"

"Well, he needs a place to sit. Look around. It's the only available spot."

"But my friend Bob got here first. It'd hardly be fair to kick him out."

Julia blinked a few times. "And where is Bob?"

"Right *there*. In the chair."

Julia blinked again as she processed the situation. "Sistine, I don't see anyone."

"Of course not. Only *I* can see Bob." She rolled her eyes. "He usually sits along the wall with his legs crossed, you know—out of the way. But he wants his *own* chair now, and you can't fault him for that. It's uncomfortable there, and he's had it with the second-class treatment."

Think, think, think. "Ummm—Bob's not a paid employee, Sistine, and Wayne, a *paid* employee, needs a desk to take calls. I'm sorry, but Bob has to move. Should I tell him, or will you?"

Sistine pouted. "I'll tell him, but he's not gonna like it."

"I appreciate your understanding." Julia walked away, stopped, and turned around. "I've always wanted to ask about your name. You have to admit it's pretty—unique."

Sistine narrowed her eyes. "My name?"

"Sistine—Chapel. As in the—Sistine Chapel?"

Sistine picked at a hangnail.

"In Rome?" Julia added.

"Never heard of it." Sistine turned to her left. "My boss says you can't sit there, Bob. I *told* you she's strict. I'll buy you some cocoa later, okay? The kind with the cute little marshmallows."

****

Mei Tanaka, the call center's no-nonsense Human Resources Rep, sat behind her desk, dressed in khaki slacks, a white polo shirt, and tennis shoes. Rectangular tortoiseshell glasses slid down her nose. Her son's framed artwork covered the walls, from a page with blue and green scribbles to a "Mom and me" stick figure drawing to a realistic rendition of an enormous gorilla climbing the Space Needle.

"Good morning. How's Kenji these days?" Julia nodded to the framed photo of a boy in a baseball uniform.

"Fine, fine. You know, 'Kenji' means 'strong' in Japanese, but I think 'strong-willed' better describes him. He's ten and acting like a teenager who knows *everything*." Mei chuckled. "How's the baby? Trey, isn't it? And how are *you*?"

"Trey's stunningly adorable and brilliant," Julia replied. "But he's still not sleeping through the night. And colic's no joke. He's getting over it, but the first six weeks were rough. I suppose I'm still adjusting." *Barely.*

Mei tapped her chest with an open hand and nodded. "I remember those days well. It gets better—I promise. So, what brings you in?"

"I'm here to talk about me, for a change, not one of my employees." Julia sucked in a long deep breath.

"I'm all ears."

Julia cleared her throat, stood up, sat down, and cleared her throat again.

"Julia? What is it?"

"It's Carlton."

Mei leaned in. "What about him?"

"Last Friday. He was, he was—inappropriate with me. And it's been going on for a long time, just not as bad."

Mei tilted her head. "What do you mean by 'inappropriate'?"

"Sexual innuendos, comments about my body, about my heritage. He says he's joking, but he's not." Julia smiled meekly. "But he went way over the line on

Friday, and I'm done brushing it off. Look, I want a promotion—I'm not afraid to admit it—and he could ruin my career, but I don't care anymore—I'm sick of him. You've gotta take him out, Mei."

Mei frowned. "Take him out?"

"I'm not talking about a *hit man* or anything. Just fire the guy. Don't let him retire with benefits. He's a good-for-nothing chauvinist pig. He grabbed my ass at Killian's Billiard Club. He asked me to suck—suck—his dick." She put her hand to her throat and suppressed the urge to barf.

"Whoa, whoa, whoa. Back up, Julia. I need specifics. *What* did Carlton say or do, *when* did he say or do it, and *who* can corroborate what you're telling me?" She looked at the clock on her desk. "Or better yet, write a statement with as much detail as you can remember. I have a meeting with the HR team from Troy Media in ten minutes."

"Oh, God. About layoffs?"

"Staffing plans, benefits, early retirement incentives, you name it. It's all on the table. If the sale goes through, we have to move out quickly. Can you have the statement to me by tomorrow? We can talk more about it then. And most importantly—do you feel safe working with Carlton, or do I need to take immediate action to separate you?"

"I can get you the statement by tomorrow, and I should be fine with Carlton—I've put up with him for years. I can do it for a while longer or avoid him altogether. And Mei, do what you can to protect my people. Where else are they going to get decent jobs with the benefits we have here?"

Mei glanced at Kenji's photo. "I'm doing my best

for all of us, but so much of this is out of my control."

****

Kelvin and Julia stood inside Carlton's empty office with the door closed. Carlton would be in all-day meetings. Phew.

"Carmen's not coming in," Kelvin said. "She spent her whole life keepin' secrets from everybody, and now that they're finally comin' out, it scares the livin' daylights out of her. And Booth's probably lookin' for her. What if he sees her come in here? I don't know if she's gonna be able to keep the job or even stay in school. It's risky."

"How about I swing by your apartment and talk to her after work tomorrow? My mother's visiting us tonight."

"I'll let Carmen know."

"How's it going for you two? I mean, you don't know her that well. Does it make you uneasy? To have a stranger living at your apartment?"

"I don't mind helpin' her out. She doesn't have anywhere to go."

"You've got a kind heart, Kelvin."

"Not when I'm dreamin' about puttin' Booth in a hammerlock and holdin' him there 'til he begs for mercy—which he ain't gonna get from me."

"A hammerlock what?"

"Wrestling move to twist him like a pretzel and hold him down."

"I approve."

Chapter Eighteen

January 25, 2017— continued

Paloma arrived at Julia and Charlie's house at four forty-five p.m. in her rented Mercedes Benz roadster convertible. Julia pulled up alongside her in the driveway. Paloma exited the car and removed a smokey blue and taupe silk scarf from her head.

Julia did a double take. "You cut your hair. I'm— I'm shocked. I never thought you'd do it."

"The hairdresser charged me ninety-six dollars to chop it off. And that's without the tip. The cost of living here is disgraceful. One avocado costs a dollar *if* it's not organic. The organic ones are two bucks apiece. Organic, my behind. Why are you tree huggers afraid of perfectly edible pesticides?"

"Don't get me wrong. Your hair looks good, but it'll take some getting used to. Now, come inside. I'll get Trey. He's asleep. The car ride does it every time." She nodded toward the backseat of her red 1996 Honda Civic with the oxidized paint on the hood and banged-up front bumper.

"Tell Carlos to get the groceries in the trunk."

"Groceries?"

"I got ingredients to make chicken enchiladas with salsa verde. I'll hold Raúl and supervise while you cook.

Or I can do the cooking."

"Charlie's not home yet, Mamá." Julia groaned as she lifted Trey's car seat from its base. "How about scrambled eggs and toast? It's been a long day."

"Aye, *Mija*. Scrambled eggs and toast? Your poor husband. I would *never* feed your father that for dinner."

"We've learned to make do with whatever we have on hand. It's too much hassle with the baby and everything."

"I can help you with the cooking when I move here."

A sour nasty taste filled Julia's mouth. She hoisted her purse and the baby bag over her shoulder, picked up the car seat, and trudged up the brick walkway toward the house.

Paloma trailed behind her. "Oh, and I bought you a car from the dealership on Highway Ninety-Nine. A sparkly gold Cadillac Escalade with a white leather interior. They're detailing it for you now. You and Carlos can pick it up tomorrow. Plenty of room for Raúl and his siblings."

Julia whipped around and stared at her mother.

"For heaven's sake, Julia. A prairie dog could hibernate in that mouth of yours." She pointed at the Honda. "That hunk of junk you call a car has to go. It's an abomination and an embarrassment. The dealership said they'd haul it away for an extra two hundred dollars, which I gladly paid. I made arrangements for them to pick it up."

Julia opened the front door and set Trey's car seat on the walkway leading to the front door. "You did *what*?"

"Go get the groceries. The car's unlocked. I'll take care of this little prince." Paloma set her Kate Spade purse on the sofa and bent over to talk to Trey. "Your *abeulita's* here, *mi amor*. Do you know how lucky you are to have me as your grandmother? You'll never want for anything, even when I'm not around." She coughed, pulled a napkin from her pocket, and held it to her mouth. "Allergies." She balled up the napkin and stuffed it in her purse. "Do all the green things around here ever stop pollinating?"

Julia took the baby bag to Trey's room and rested her back against the wall. *She bought us a car. She cut her hair.*

"*Mija*," Paloma called. "Get Raúl out of this contraption so we can visit each other cheek to cheek. They make these newfangled things so complicated to use."

"I'll take him out after I get the groceries." *It's like I'm ten years old again. Next, she'll tell me to pick her nose for her, and I'll probably do it.*

****

"She did *what*?" Charlie hissed in the bedroom as he changed into gray lounge pants and a "Nacho Average Teacher" T-shirt with a pile of chips, cheese sauce, and jalapeño slices on the back. "I know she means well, but your car still runs fine. It needs a coat of paint. So what? And a Cadillac Escalade? It's a gas guzzler. We would never have bought that, even if we did have the money. She's generous, I'll give her that, but she's so—pushy."

Julia climbed onto the bed and crisscrossed her legs. "From her perspective, what she wants is best. Period. Full stop. And why would she bother with anyone else's opinion if she knows she's one hundred percent right one hundred percent of the time? That woman confounds me. I'd be happy if she said, 'I love you, Julia,' but no, she goes off and buys us a Cadillac." She rubbed her chin. "It's a different way of showing affection, but she still drives me batshit crazy."

"So, what do we do about the Cadillac?" Charlie asked.

"Tell her to shove it up her butt?"

"Or swallow our pride and accept it. We can trade it for something more practical and fuel-efficient in a few years. How much longer do you think she's going to stay?"

"She said she's going to move here."

Charlie put his hand to his forehead as if a headache was coming on. "Hmph. At least we'll have a babysitter nearby. Your mother loves you, Julia. She just wants to be near you and the baby."

"I don't think that's it. Something weird's going on."

****

Charlie did the dishes and retreated to the family room with Trey to watch a rerun of the Seattle Seahawks' win against the San Francisco 49ers.

"The enchiladas were delish, honey," he called out.

"I made the black bean salad," Paloma said through the arched doorway.

"Of course. The black bean salad was *fannnn-tastic*, Paloma," he said.

"Of course it was," Paloma replied.

Paloma and Julia went to the small kitchen with the turquoise and yellow backsplash tiles and daisy wallpaper from the 1960s. Julia pulled out the ingredients to make *pan de polvo*, crispy, melt-in-your-mouth cookies full of cinnamon, anise, and vanilla.

"You said you're making these for an employee of

yours?" Paloma asked. "Is it her birthday?"

"I'm going to visit her tomorrow. She's in a tough situation, and I thought the cookies might cheer her up. Her mother's from Mexico, so these should be familiar to her."

"Where in Mexico?"

"She never said."

"How long has, has—what's the employee's name?" Paloma made her way to the kitchen table, breathing in short choppy spurts before sitting down.

"What's up with your breathing?"

"It doesn't take much to tire me out these days. I'm probably anemic again—nothing some iron supplements can't fix."

"You're not that old, Mamá. You should get checked out. I can give you my doctor's name if you want to make an appointment. And, the employee's name is Carmen Cooper."

"Doctors who practice in Podunk towns do so because they're not qualified for reputable hospitals and clinics—like in Dallas and Houston. And Carmen Cooper? That hardly sounds like a Mexican name—kind of like—Trey."

Julia dumped the shortening into a mixing bowl. "Does it matter what her name is, Mamá?"

"How long has she worked for you?"

"About a month."

"I presume you do this for all your employees, then?"

Julia measured the sugar, dumped it in the bowl, and pulled the vanilla from a cabinet. "Why the inquisition? I'm making cookies for an employee. Is that so weird?"

Paloma flashed her "if looks could kill" eyes. "I do

not like your tone. What's gotten into you?"

Julia's nostrils flared. "You showed up unannounced and bought us a Cadillac without asking, that's what."

"Julia María Navarro. How can you be so ungrateful? Tell me you want me to go, and I'll go because I will not be treated like S-H-I-T by my own daughter."

Julia turned on the mixer, and sugar flew everywhere. "Dammit. I turned it on too high." She grabbed a paper towel and ran it under the faucet. "I don't mean to treat you like S-H-I-T, otherwise known as shit. I know you're trying to do the right thing, but I wish you'd consult me before you make decisions that affect my life." She got on her hands and knees and wiped up the far-flung sugar.

"Well, words have consequences, *Mija*. I came here for a reason—I wasn't just *in the area*. I'll leave without hesitation if you continue to talk to me with disrespect or if I feel unwanted."

Julia squeezed the back of her neck. "I'm sorry, Mamá. The baby, my boss, and a complicated situation with this employee have me completely stressed out." Julia pulled out a chair across from her mother, sat, and dropped her head into her hands. "Most days feel like I'm walking through floodwater."

"Yes, well, the rain here *is* legendary."

Julia grabbed her mother's hand across the table. "I'm sorry I got angry with you. You said you came here for a reason. What did you mean?"

"I want to get to know my grandson and help you. Let me take care of Raúl while you're at work—avoid the daycare altogether. Wouldn't that take a load off your shoulders and save money? Talk it over with Carlos. I can get here in the morning and stay as long as you need. I thought I saw a house with a for-sale sign the next street over, although the housing prices here are outrageous. Not that I can't afford it. If you want me to buy it, just say the word."

Julia stood up and hugged her mother for the first time in—in—she couldn't remember how long. Paloma stiffened and patted her daughter's back with a rigid hand.

"Now, tell me more about this employee of yours," Paloma said, standing and smoothing out the wrinkles in the apron tied around her waist.

Maybe Julia's exhaustion weakened her defenses. Maybe she needed some mothering of her own, even if it came from her actual mother. She told Paloma everything about Carmen. And the two women, as different as high and low, soft and hard, hot and cold, a Cadillac Escalade and beat-up Honda, devised a plan to join forces to save Carmen and bring Booth to justice.

Could my life get any weirder? Julia wondered. *My mother and I are collaborating on something.*

****

With Charlie and Trey asleep, and her mother back at her beachside bed and breakfast, Julia sat at the kitchen table in her leggings, Hard Rock Café sweatshirt, and bunny slippers. The cold came through the hazy single-pane glass window. She drew a frown face in the condensation trickling into tiny puddles inside the window track and opened her laptop. The words came fast and furious—a vein in her jugular pulsed.

January 25, 2017
To Whom It May Concern,

My employment began at The Chronicle on July 25, 2008. In May 2014, I got a management position in the call center under the leadership of Carlton Cressey. Since that time, I have experienced ongoing harassment of a sexual and racist nature. During my first one-on-one meeting with Carlton, he said he chose me for the job because he liked my "chi-chis." He refers to me as a "hot Mexican mama," his "spicy little Lolita," and his "favorite call girl." He comments on what I'm wearing, my weight, and my body parts at least once a week. I have asked him to stop multiple times. He insists that he's joking to justify his behavior.

On Friday, January 20, 2017, I met Carlton at Killian's Billiard Club at his invitation. He told me key senior leaders would be there and that, given his imminent retirement, I would be wise to network with them. No other senior leaders were there, and I'm convinced they never got invited. The names Carlton mentioned were Mitchell Manion, Al Carmichael, and Doug Norman—you could check with them to verify.

Already alcohol-impaired when I arrived, Carlton grabbed my buttocks and asked me to "have some fun tonight," "help him find that loving feeling," and commit a sex act. He also implied that he would not select me for a promotion if I didn't do as he asked. I walked out.

As I think back on the harassment, I cannot recall a time when he did it in the presence of other Chronicle employees, so, to my knowledge, there are no witnesses on or off-premises (except for the Killian's bartender).

I regret not bringing this to your attention sooner. I regret going along with it for the sake of my career and out of embarrassment. I want Carlton Cressey held accountable for breaking The Chronicle's Code of

Conduct and no-tolerance policy on harassment. Please let me know what else you need beyond this written statement.

Sincerely,
Julia Navarro-Nilsson

Chapter Nineteen

January 26, 2017
The Cascade City Chronicle

"Racquetball Club for Seniors Canceled as Contusion Injuries Mount"

Streaks of moonlight came through the clouds. Carmen instructed the driver to leave her on the roadside near the mailboxes. The wind whistled through the frost-laden rhododendron bushes. She pulled Kelvin's black puffy coat in close, tucked her freezing hands under her armpits, and walked up the long, curved driveway in the dark, thankful for the little bit of translucent light. She absolutely, unequivocally could not be discovered. If Booth found her there, things could turn deadly, especially if he was drunk.

She stared at the house for a minute, or what she could see of it. *Mami needs me*, she told herself. *Keep going. Don't chicken out.*

Her mother's bedroom appeared dark—not unexpected at two o'clock in the morning. She pushed herself through the bare branches of an overgrown Japanese maple, formed a knuckle, and tapped the window pane softly.

Nothing.

She turned on the tiny flashlight hanging from a key

chain, shined it through the glass, and tapped again.

The curtains parted, and the window slid open a crack.

"Carmen?" her mother whispered.

Carmen stepped in closer. "*Si, Mami.*"

"Turn off the light. Where did you go? I've been worried sick."

"I'm staying with a friend. Are *you* okay?"

"He threatened to call the *coyote.*"

"Mami, he threatens that all the time. Does he know where I am?"

"No, and it's driving him mad. He thinks you will contact the police if you haven't already, and he can't have me here when they show up. The *coyote* will search for you, too. He can make a lot of money by selling us to the narcos." Consuelo put her finger to her lips and turned slightly. "Shhh. I hear something," she whispered and hurried away.

Carmen crouched below the windowsill, ready to jump and run.

She waited ten minutes, but her mother did not return.

****

Julia peeked into Mei Tanaka's office. "Good morning."

Mei looked up from her stack of papers. "Hi." Mei smiled. "You bring that letter for me?"

Julia handed her an envelope. Mei read the letter and ran her hands through her short hair.

"I'll get started on this today, but honestly, there's not much to go on," Mei said. "With no witnesses, it'll be your word against Carlton's unless he admits to it—which he won't. These cases can be frustrating for all involved."

"But it's true—I assure you. Every word."

"Just because we can't prove something doesn't mean it didn't happen. My job is to investigate this objectively. Gather the facts. Decide whether there's been a policy violation and recommend a course of action. Carlton reports to Tim Akers, right?"

Julia nodded.

"Have you ever mentioned this to Tim?"

"No. What was I supposed to do? Tell him that Carlton likes my jugs? No way. The only people besides you who know are Jerry Dean and my husband."

"Good to know. I may reach out to Jerry. Let me know if anything else comes up."

****

A delivery truck drove into a ditch, and a swath of Cascade City had no newspaper. Call volumes ballooned. And with a headline like "Racquetball Club for Seniors Canceled as Contusion Injuries Mount," who wouldn't get pissed off about a missed delivery? Rumor had it the truck driver had a prostitute in the cab conducting a "testicle inspection" at the time of the incident.

Julia walked the floor to ensure everyone on the schedule was taking calls. "It's going to be one of those days," she told Kelvin. "Busy as all get out. It's always something. That's the fun of the newspaper business, though. It's a circus, but I like juggling. Or I did when I was still good at it. I can't even juggle *imaginary* balls these days."

"Ya want me to take calls?" Kelvin asked. "I don't mind."

"I may take you up on it if it stays like this for long.

How's Carmen?"

"All right, I guess."

"Does she know I'm coming this afternoon?"

"Yes, ma'am. The last thing she needs is surprises right now. I'll be home by then, so I'll be with y'all."

"Kelvin? I've been talking to Jerry in the newsroom, and…"

Kelvin frowned. "Noooo. You were supposed to keep it secret. You promised."

"It's gonna take more than the two of us to help her. We're going to solve this thing." Julia twisted her wedding ring round and round a few times and stared at the wall, picturing all the things that could go wrong.

****

Carmen sat on the sofa in Kelvin's apartment. She set her mushy cereal on the coffee table and opened her diary.

Ninth Grade

February 14, 2012

Dear Monica,

I thought I might start finally addressing you as Dear Diary but why bother changing now? Monica works. If it ain't broke, don't fix it right? Except my stupid life feels broke and it needs fixing. I asked a sophomore (!) named Austin Collier to TOLO, and he turned me down. He's already going with Tessa Mayfield, a blonde girl with freckles. I was nervous to try again, but I asked another boy, Noah Taylor-Adams, and he said no too. He said he'd be out of town that night visiting his granma, but he said yes to Lauren Pritchett the next day. What's wrong with me? Do I smell or something? Am I that ugly? I'm not popular maybe because I look different or because I'm short? Do kids think I'm stuckup because I'm quiet? I don't play sports. Papa Percy says I could get hurt, and he won't take me to doctor or a hospital, and he won't put up with any crying if a bone gets broken. Doctors ask too many questions he said. I can't join choir because it costs money to go on trips to other schools. I know he has enough money. It's school and home, school and home. My life's boring and sad sad sad. But he said I can go to college IF I get a scholarship. Mami is so so so happy about that. She never got past 3rd grade. I want to be a writer someday, then I can write about another world much better than this one.

Papa took one of his guns onto the porch. He heard noises in the bushes and thought someone was watching us maybe the police or some guys from Hollywood. Or it could be someone from his fan club. They knock on the door sometimes wanting an autograph. Those people are nutty. When he couldn't find anyone making the noises he went to Dorthea's room and talked to her like he always does. She's dead, but Mami and me don't say it anymore. He whipped me with the belt buckle last time I told him Dorthea can't hear him. And he wouldn't let me eat for two days. He locks the pantry and the refrigerator and only he knows the code. Sometimes he makes Mami go three or four days without eating except the food she hides when she cooks for him. Once he found crackers in her pocket and hit her so hard it broke her nose and it looked crooked after that. He broke my nose once but that was a long time ago and my nose angles a little to the right. Or maybe it's more crooked than I think and thats why boys won't go to TOLO with me. I wish I knew. What do I do to be popular? Maybe I should dye my hair blonde.

Sincerely,
Carmen Camacho, my real name

She left Kelvin's apartment and walked around the corner to Russell's Pawn Shop. The guy in the skull T-shirt behind the counter bought the Victorian-era horseshoe brooch with thirty-six tiny sapphires that Papa Percy stole from the set of *The Gunslinger* and that she took from Dorthea's jewelry box and hid in her backpack. The gun she bought with the money from the brooch left her two hundred and fifty dollars to spare, fifty of which she used to buy herself an old-model flip phone.

Chapter Twenty

January 26, 2017—continued

At two o'clock in the afternoon, Paloma sashayed into the daycare wearing a lilac linen dress, white cashmere cardigan, pearls, and white blinged-out slingback pumps. Betty from the infant room greeted Paloma. Betty's soft white curls framed her round face and rosy cheeks.

"It's nice to meet you, Ms. Navarro. Your grandson's right here." Betty opened a second door to a room that smelled of dirty diapers and baby powder. "He sure is a cute one."

Paloma cocked her head. "Of *course* he is. I'm sure he's the most handsome boy in the entire place."

Raúl lay in a bouncy seat, his chubby legs kicking the air.

Paloma's eyes softened at the edges. "He's—well, he's gorgeous." She smiled at her grandson. "He looks exactly like *me*."

Betty blinked a few times. "Yes, ma'am, he sure does."

Paloma clasped her hands. "You'd never know he's half Norwegian. Such cold people up there."

"I thought Charlie's family emigrated from Stockholm. I only remember that because my own family's from Sollentuna, just north of there. In the 1850s, my grandfather set out…"

"Did my daughter leave Raúl's car seat for me?"

"It's right over here." Betty pointed to a wall with a line of car seats against it. "Wait. Did you say, 'Raúl?' "

Paloma fluttered her eyelashes. "Yes, I prefer to call him by his masculine Mexican name. Be a dear and put him in that contraption for me."

"Oh—gosh. I've got a bad hip, but I'll do my best."

Paloma watched the older woman bend over and fumble around until she connected the straps and clicked the belt between Raúl's legs.

Betty put her hand on her lower back and slowly stood up. "Usually, the parents do this," she said, her face flushed.

"Now, carry it out for me. By the way, I *love* your tennis shoes with that yellow polka dot dress. Did you get them at a secondhand store? I hear those places have good deals. Of course, I've never shopped at one."

Betty enlisted the daycare's young cook to carry the bulky car seat outside and hook it into the rental car. Paloma reached in and ran her hand over Trey's head. "Such soft, beautiful curls. I'm envious of an infant— can you believe that?"

"I'm sorry; what did you say?" Betty asked.

"My hair used to be the envy of every girl in Laredo." Paloma ran her fingers across her head. A black clump fell. "My goodness, where are my manners?" She wiped hairs off her shoulders, opened her purse, pulled out a hundred-dollar bill, and pushed it into Betty's hand.

Betty's mouth went slack. "Is this a tip? We don't take tips, Mrs. Navarro, but thank you kindly." She extended her arm with the bill in her hand.

"Keep it. I'm richer than God." Paloma started the car and peeled out of the parking lot.

****

Julia stood outside apartment number three-o-eight for a full minute before she knocked. She pulled a bottle of water from her bag and took a swig, leaving her craving something stiffer.

Kelvin opened the door. "Welcome."

Carmen stood behind him in gray sweatpants, flip-flops, and an Oklahoma Christian College sweatshirt that hung on her like a mini-dress.

"Thank you," Julia replied. "I brought some cookies for you." She held out a container. "*Pan de polvo.* Have you had these before, Carmen?"

"Oh, yes. Well, at least *I* have," Carmen answered. "Mami makes them at Christmastime."

Kelvin took the cookies and set them on the kitchen counter. "Can I getcha somethin' to drink?" he asked Julia. "I have orange juice and milk, though I don't advise drinkin' 'em together—it'll taste like vomit if ya do that. And I have water. Of course, I have water."

"No, thanks. I've got something with me," Julia said, motioning to the baby bag slung over her shoulder. Carmen looked toward Julia with a distant gaze and a pasted-on smile. *Start with small talk. Get her comfortable with me.* "I used to laugh at moms who carried one of these frumpy things as a purse, but you can't argue with the efficiency of it." She laughed. *Keep it light.* "I hope you enjoy the cookies. My mother made them at Christmastime, too." She waited for Carmen to chime in, like, "I love the cinnamon sugar," or, "I'd eat them year-round if I could." But no. Carmen walked to the sofa, sat on the edge, and sighed. *So much for small talk.* Julia nodded toward a weathered wicker rocking chair. "Okay to sit?"

"Of course," Kelvin replied, lowering himself onto the sofa next to Carmen.

"Carmen, we don't know each other well, and you're taking a leap of faith here—thank you for trusting me," Julia said. "I promise I only want to help." She shrugged her shoulders. "My husband advised me to stay away from this, but I think a terrible injustice is happening, and it hurts my heart. Jerry Dean from the newsroom is helping me. We'll do everything we can to get you and your mom away from Booth and hold him accountable for what he's done. What I need from you is to fill in the details. We have to prove what he's done is illegal."

"You can't get the authorities involved. If that's what you're planning, I'll do this alone," Carmen stammered. "We don't have papers. Percy took Mami's the day he brought her here. Even if Mami has evidence that she's in danger, she can't claim asylum—it's not enough. They'll deport us for sure. I don't even have a birth certificate. Mami delivered me by herself in the house."

Kelvin set his hand on Carmen's shoulder. "You should tell Julia why your mother can't go back to Mexico."

"My parents worked in a governor's house. Mami cleaned, and Papi was the groundskeeper. The governor was threatening to crack down on the drug cartels. Men with rifles stormed the house and shot the governor in his bed. Mami and Papi were there when it happened. They killed my Papi a week later. The governor's wife disappeared a few days after that. They hanged her from a street light in the middle of town. Mami had nowhere to go. A man called 'Spider' promised her a good job in America. She didn't know someone had paid him to smuggle her across the border. Percy Booth *bought* my mother. She got here in a truck smooshed in with forty-eight other people."

Julia gulped a swig of water. *Fuckity fuck fuck. I'm way over my head here.* "Jerry and I won't call the authorities for now, but if we find out your mother is in immediate danger, we'll have to."

Carmen nodded and wiped tears with the sleeve of her sweatshirt.

"Jerry's working on getting you legal help," Julia continued. "I assume you want Booth prosecuted to the full extent of the law?"

The gold streaks in Carmen's eyes flickered. "I want him to rot in jail."

Julia pulled the reporter's notebook out of the baby bag. "Let's get started, then. Jerry gave this to me." She held up the spiral-bound notebook. "A laptop's too bulky to carry with all the other stuff in here: diapers, butt wipes, change of clothes, the kitchen sink." She fished out a hard case with two perfectly sharpened pencils inside. "First things first. Does Booth know where you are?"

"No. I asked Mami last night."

Kelvin jerked his head back. "You did what?"

"Forgive me, but I had to know if she was okay. You were sleeping when I left."

Kelvin rubbed his cheek and left the room. He came back holding a beer. "Take me with you if you need to see her again. I can't protect you if I'm not there."

Carmen stroked his arm. "Thank you."

****

After an hour of question and answer, Julia called Jerry on the drive home. Fluffy cotton candy clouds stirred overhead.

"Jer? I just talked to Carmen, and I have *a lot* to tell you. Plus, my mother and I hatched a plan, and I want to know what you think."

"You? And Paloma? Working together?"

"Stranger things have happened."

"Like what?"

"Pet rocks?"

"Good one."

"Jerry?"

"Huh?"

"Part of me wants to put my head under the covers and suck my thumb."

"None of that. Do you hear me? We can do this. I have an idea for getting Consuelo out of there."

Julia's shoulders loosened. "Thank God."

****

Julia decided to save the Cadillac dealership a trip and stopped by to pick up the new car. She grudgingly left her Honda Civic behind and drove home in the white Escalade (color: "stardust," Paloma's pick). Seattleites preferred fuel-efficient, all-wheel-drive cars with sports racks on top for mountain bikes, skis, camping gear, etc. But in Cascade City, where half the population consisted of loaded retirees, the Escalade fit right in.

She arranged for her and Charlie to have dinner at Mama Mendoza's while Paloma babysat. She'd tell him everything *after* he had a few drinks. No more keeping him in the dark.

****

They sat in a booth. Julia set a white paper sack from an electronics store by her feet.

"Do you remember the night of our freshman year's talent show and the cast party afterward?" Charlie asked. "We went to Joe Crenshaw's house and sat in two of those expensive bean bag chairs you buy at the mall. It's amazing how doing something as innocuous as choosing a place to sit can turn out to be a life-changer."

"I knew that night that I'd marry you one day," Julia said. "And so did every other girl in that room."

Charlie blushed. "How could you know that? We'd only known each other for two months."

Julia smoothed and straightened the dinner napkin on her lap and pulled the silverware into perfect vertical alignment. "I thought you were rich." She winked at him.

"Hah! I thought I was rich, too, or that I *would be* when Aunt Astrid passed. She raised me, after all. I guess she decided the art museum needed the money more than I did."

"She never forgave you for marrying a mouthy Mexican with a watch repairman for a father and a mom who grew up hawking gum and newspapers at the border crossing. She cut you out of the will as punishment."

"Aunt Astrid was a snooty ole lady, but she loved me, Julia. My mom was her favorite niece. When she died, Astrid didn't hesitate to take me in as her own. She didn't like that I became a teacher either. Ruined her plan to tell her rich friends she raised a brain surgeon or supreme court justice or something."

"Uh-huh," Julia chuckled. "I should have kicked your booty to the curb after the inheritance fell through. Your good looks saved you."

"But the sex was too good, right?"

153

"Ohhhh, yeaaahhh. That was it." A cascade of images flashed in Julia's memory bank of juicy lovemaking on the sofa (sitting position), the living room floor (a little scratchy on the area rug), in the car (front and back seats), on top of the toilet seat (closed), and an upstairs bedroom at a friend's potluck dinner (hot!).

The smile on Charlie's face went flat. "Honey, I miss us. Not just the sex but our talks and watching our shows together before bed. I mean, we're way behind on a bunch of them. The teachers at school are talking about *Beal Street Law*, and I'm lost. Something big happened to Cora, the attorney general, but the teachers won't give me any details." Charlie rolled his shoulders in little circles and tilted his head from right to left. "I miss going to see the tulips in Skagit Valley. I miss wine tasting in Woodinville, making dinner together, and talking about the books we've read. Hell, I haven't read a book since November. Remember when we used to hang out at bars and shoot pool until they closed the place? I love Trey more than I imagined, but you and I have drifted apart since he was born. It's not his fault, of course, and I'm sure other parents go through the same thing, but we've got to work harder, babe. I don't want to go on like this."

"What do you mean 'you don't want to go on…' "

A guy with "Alberto" on his name tag approached.

"*Hola, amigos.* Can I start you off with some drinks? Margaritas? Extra large with the best tequila?"

Julia used her cloth napkin to wipe away a tear. "I'll have lemonade."

"A shot of tequila, *muy grande*, *por favor*," Charlie said, sounding as Gringo as ever.

"I'll bring your drinks and take the rest of your order," Alberto said.

Julia let the tears go. "I agree with you, babe." She moved around to Charlie's side of the booth and rested her head on his shoulder. "I'm so worn out and overwhelmed with the baby, work, and things I haven't even told you yet. But there's no excuse—guilty as charged. I wanted us to be alone tonight to talk—to tell you what's happening with me. I'm in deep shit with something at work. You should know about it in case I get into trouble."

"Get into trouble?" Charlie asked, shifting his position.

"And about the sex, Jesus H Christ, I'm truly sorry, but my libido's gone the way of Jimmy Hoffa, buried somewhere, probably in Jersey. It has to be a hormone thing, and I'm sure it won't last forever. I shaved my crotch yesterday, if that makes you feel any better. All the porn stars do it. I wanted to surprise you with it tonight, although, fair warning—I've got stubble down there. You could get road rash on your face, and what would you tell your students?"

"C'mon, honey, you know I'll take my chances with the road rash. What did you mean about getting into trouble?"

"What's with the faces?" Ana asked, strolling toward them, her black skirt embroidered with a peacock design swishing across the floor. "You look like Mopey the Clown," she said to Julia. "And you look like you just saw a two-headed Chihuahua," she told Charlie. "Well, there's nothing good fajitas can't fix. Can you smell them? We use real mesquite from Home Depot. And our onions are charred to perfection. Best fajitas in town. Best fajitas in Seattle. These Northwesterners can't do Mexican food for shit—pardon my French. People come from as far away as Portland to eat our fajitas. Oregon. Not Maine."

"I see you put the signs out." Julia nodded toward a white tent card on the table, reading, *Please note: Ongoing thefts have led to the installation of recording devices throughout this establishment. If you do not wish to be recorded, you must notify management.* "The equipment I mentioned is right here." She grabbed the white paper bag by her feet. "Thank you for helping us."

"Yes, of course. I'll have Alberto set it up after we close. I want to catch the bastard as much as you do—at whatever it is that he's doing. I'm sure he'll be in tomorrow with Senator Mathis. They never miss the half-off Friday lunch special. Cheap bastards. Neither one leaves a tip."

Charlie's mouth hung open like a fish mid-bubble. He looked at Julia, then Ana, and back again. "Ana, can you get me that tequila shot now?"

The left side of Ana's mouth lifted in half a smile. "It pleases me to serve you, Carlos."

"Ana? *Dos, por favor*?" Charlie held up two fingers. "Julia? What in the hell is going on here? I am freaking out. In case you get into trouble? And what's in that bag? I wanted more excitement in our lives, but this isn't what I had in mind."

"Maybe I should tell you at home. It's too noisy here. I'll tell Alberto to bag up the food."

"We'll go home *after* the shots, and you can drive." He shook his head. "What in the hell have you been keeping from me?"

****

Julia sent her mother back to The Beachcomber. She and Charlie lay in bed facing each other—him in his boxer briefs, her a baggy T-shirt with Jovita Idar, a Mexican journalist and activist, on the front.

"I like to think I'm pretty easygoing, but what is happening?" Charlie asked. "I'm already feeling angry and don't even know what it is yet."

"It's Carmen—the employee at work. Do you remember when I checked on her at her house, and Percy Booth came out with a gun?"

"How could I forget that? I wanted you to call the cops."

"Jerry and I are trying to prove that he's holding Carmen and her mother against their will."

"Wait. What? And you still haven't called the police?"

"We need to figure out how to keep Carmen and her mother from getting deported. They don't have papers or a valid asylum claim. Jerry's trying to find them a lawyer who'll take the case pro bono."

Charlie sat up. "It's not your responsibility to save this young woman or her mother. I applaud that you *want* to, but we've got a son to raise, and—I can't do it without you. What if something goes wrong? You're dealing with a gunslinger who's off his rocker. You're a call center manager, for Christ's sake."

"Jerry and I have a plan. And my mother's going to help."

"You're kidding–your mother's involved? Are *you* off your rocker? I'm not happy about this, Julia. Not happy at all. And how come everybody knows but me?"

"I didn't want you to worry. It was wrong of me not to tell you."

"Uh-huh. It was wrong of you. You're my wife, and we made a promise to each other. We don't keep secrets—or at least I thought we didn't." Charlie got out of bed, pulled on a pair of sweatpants, and left the room.

"Charlie? Where are you going?"

"To watch TV. Alone."

An hour later, Julia tiptoed into the family room topless. It was a shameless try at making amends, but she didn't know what else to do.

"Sorry, babe," she said. "I know I screwed up."

"I'm sure you're doing this to help Carmen, to do your part in ridding the world of injustice. I admire that—I do. But you can't shut me out. We're partners for life. No more secrets. You promise?"

"Yes. I promise." She moved in closer and leaned down to kiss him. He took a nipple in his mouth instead.

Chapter Twenty-One

January 27, 2017
The Cascade City Chronicle

"LoveLine Channel to Shoot *Sun, Sand, and Secrets* in Cascade City This February"
At six a.m., Paloma sat in a deep green wingback chair in her room overlooking the beach and dialed the Dallas Methodist Oncology Center. The doctor said she would refer Paloma to Seattle's Fred Hutchinson Cancer Center for continued chemotherapy treatment, although tests showed it wasn't making much difference.
After her morning coffee, *pain au chocolate*, and a thorough reading of the wimpy local paper, she contacted the Director of St. Luke's Parish. Using the name 'Carol Martin,' she expressed an interest in donating to their new school fund—perhaps enough to build an adjacent community theatre the schoolchildren could use. But before committing to any such sizeable gift, she insisted on a one-on-one meeting with board president, retired senator Emerson Mathis. The senator, she demanded, must speak with her at the Beachcomber Bed and Breakfast at three p.m. sharp.
"You see," she said, "it's now or never."
****
Julia walked through the newsroom on her lunch

break.

Millie Meeks, the newsroom's battle-ax receptionist, a Chronicle fixture for five decades, got up from her desk and looked squarely at Julia.

"You make any of them fancy hazelnut brownies lately?" she asked. "Ya see this?" She pointed with her arthritic big-knuckled finger. "I got coffee and nothing to go with it."

"Sorry, Millie. I haven't baked in ages. I'll try to bring you something next week, okay?"

"Yeah, yeah. That doesn't help me now. You used to bring me ass-fattening stuff all the time. But listen here. Don't get your panties in a twist over anything I say. I went to frozen dinners when my Fergus was born. Me and Swanson TV dinners got a thing goin'—the meatloaf's not bad, and that little cup of apple cobbler on the side? Hot damn, that shit's good."

"You know where Jerry is, Millie?"

"Jerry?" She wrinkled her nose. "Who can keep track of that guy? He's probably watching a movie or something—tough job. I wanna watch movies and eat out for a living, too. That guy can kiss my ass, and you can tell him I said so."

The multiline phone rang on Millie's desk. "Chronicle. Whaddya want?" she answered.

Julia waved goodbye and continued her search past the features desk, the tiny test kitchen, and the editorial department. The cluttered mess covering every inch of the newsroom made her want to dive into a vat of antibacterial gel. She pulled out her cell phone.

—*Where are you?*— she texted Jerry.

—*Lactation room*— he texted back.

—*WTF?*—

—*Im milking the unstructured nature of my job. LOL.*—

—*Funny har-har. And you forgot the apostrophe in I'm.*—

—*Bitch*—

—*You forgot the period after bitch.*—

—*Shut up and come find me. We've gotta talk.*—

—*Gotta's not a real word.*—

—*Neither   is   get-your-hiney-over-here-or-im-gonna-kick-it-from-here-to-Timbuktu*—

Julia walked toward the composing room, where a couple of page designers laid out final news copy, headlines, ads, and graphics on a computer.

She tapped on the door with one finger.

Jerry opened it an inch and peered out. "Get in here."

"What are you doing?"

Jerry latched the door behind her. "Watching Percy Booth in *Sheriff of Chaco Canyon*." He wore a ruffled shimmery silver tuxedo shirt, boots, and jeans so tight he had to have laid down to shimmy into them.

"Why in the mother's room, of all places?"

"Duh." He pursed his lips. "I'm hiding."

"What's up, Jer?"

"It's a Percy Booth movie marathon in here—part of my research as a hard-hitting undercover reporter. Marcus still doesn't know—I don't like him telling me what I can and can't do."

"He is your boss, you know. That's what bosses do."

"And your point is? Look, the last thing I want is for him to catch on to what we're doing. My big break hangs in the balance, and Marcus Manseau, my editor with a burr up his ass and a mind as tight as Fort Knox, will not ruin it."

"The voice recorder got put under Booth and Mathis' table at Mama Mendoza's last night. And Ana put up signs about recordings taking place to catch would-be thieves." Julia winked.

"That was a great fucking idea, Julia."

"Yeah, well, we'll see what turns up. Hopefully, they'll say something incriminating at their usual Friday lunch. And my mother will work on Mathis separately."

Jerry clicked the pause button on an image of Percy Booth on a galloping horse amid various sizes of desert cacti, presumably in Chaco Canyon, but most likely on a set in L.A. "So here's my latest stroke of genius. I talked to Stanford, Booth's stepson, yesterday. He swears that the revolver Booth had the day you met him on his porch is one he stole from a movie set. It's not a replica—it's an original 1876 Colt single-action revolver used in Bandido in the Badlands, Booth's last movie with Spectacle Studios. The props guy bought it from some down-on-his-luck rancher near Mexico City and used it in the film. I looked it up—it's worth a hundred thousand bucks now. The studio reported it stolen back in the day but never recovered it. Percy bragged about it to Stanford—get this—after threatening to shoot Stanford with it. What possessed Percy to steal shit from movie sets, I'll never understand.

"The plan is for Stanford to report the stolen revolver to the police," Jerry continued, "and when they show up at the house on Overlook Drive, and Booth's dealing with that, Consuelo will escape through the back door and meet me in the alley. I'll be waiting in my car. The police won't know anything about Consuelo or Carmen, so that shouldn't be an issue." Jerry leaned back in his chair, huffed a warm breath onto his fingernails, and rubbed them on his tuxedo shirt.

Julia held up her index finger. "Wait. Booth drinks himself into a stupor regularly. He goes out to lunch every Friday. Consuelo could have escaped any number of times. How will this plan of yours work? How do you know she'll leave?"

"Carmen has to tell Consuelo that if she doesn't walk out the back door on cue, we'll notify the police that she's in there. And isn't that what she's afraid of the most? Law enforcement?"

"That seems harsh. To threaten Consuelo like that?"

"We have to, Julia. She's in danger, and he's an asshole who should spend the rest of his life at the prison with the other thugs. You have any better ideas?"

Julia chewed on the inside of her cheek. "No, I guess not."

"You feel it? The electricity in the air? Ole Percy's about to get busted. Tell me I'm brilliant. You know I am."

"I need to get in touch with Carmen. She has to let her mother know."

Jerry frowned. "You don't want to say I'm brilliant?"

"Yeah. I don't want to say it." Julia leaned over to kiss Jerry's cheek. "But you sure are cute."

"Juan Carlos tells me I'm cute all the time."

"How is Juan Carlos?"

"He moved in with me."

"As long as you're happy, Jer."

"He's an attorney. Makes good money. Smokin' hot in bed. Sexy accent. What's not to be happy about? And he's trying to find an attorney for Consuelo and Carmen– a free one. He could be a keeper, Julia."

"I'll let you know what comes of the voice recorder at Mama Mendoza's."

"And I'll tell you after Stanford calls the police about the revolver. Have Carmen tell her mother tonight, so there's no surprise."

"Jer?"

"Mmm?"

"Where will Consuelo stay?"

"You expect me to have *all* the answers?" He tapped his chin. "How about your place?"

"Very funny, Jer. That's a good one."

****

Julia rounded the corner on her way to the stairwell and smacked into someone the size of a fridge coming the other way. "Fuckity-fuck. I'm sorry!" Julia exclaimed, clutching her chest and looking up at the face of the refrigerator. "Jesus H Christ, you're tall."

The man wore a gray suit, a deep purple tie, and sleek silver-rimmed glasses. Patches of white at the temples touched off his thick dark hair.

"Six feet eight inches, to be exact," the man said. "Cleveland Cavaliers, power forward, 1983-1987," he offered. "Not that I'm bragging. I sat on the bench more than I'd like to admit." The man stuck out his right hand. "I'm Bennett Keller."

"Oh. Fuckity-fuck." Julia gasped. "I'm Julia—Julia—Navarro—Nil…" Julia's brain powered down for a second. "Julia Navarro-Nilsson. From the call center. I work in your call center. *The* call center, 'cause it's not *your* call center, now is it? Or maybe it *is your* call center. You're Bob Keller's son. As in, Bob Keller. You know. The publisher?"

"That's right," he replied, "except I'm the publisher

and CEO now. Dad retired last May."

"Pfft. Of course. I knew that." Julia smiled weakly. "I work here."

"So you said. Would you like to come to my office? I haven't gotten to know anyone from the call center except Carlton. Last name, 'Creepy,' isn't it? Carlton Creepy? And I hear he's retiring soon."

"Hah!" Julia laughed. "Did you do that on purpose?"

"His last name's not Creepy?" Bennett smirked.

"It's Cressey."

"Honest mistake. Come with me." Bennett beckoned toward the executive suite where Julia had never stepped foot. "I've got twenty minutes until my next meeting. If you have time, why don't you give me the short version of Call Center 101? I've worked here since I was fifteen but still have much to learn."

Oh my God, he's the publisher.

Do I tell him that Creepy Cressey wants to get in my pants?

Hell no.

Maybe start with, "How about them Seahawks?"

Bad idea. You don't speak football.

Or, "What about them Sonics?"

No, stupid. Oklahoma City stole the Seattle Sonics years ago, and you don't speak basketball.

The two walked into a luxurious room with pine forest green-colored walls, lush cream carpet, bookshelves packed with leather-bound titles, velvety barrel chairs, silk flower arrangements, a Washington State flag, northwest art by Mark Tobey, Jacob Lawrence, and Kenneth Callahan, and a coffee station complete with an espresso machine, and pineapple-shaped shortbread cookies dipped in chocolate.

"Maggie? I'll be in my office with Julie Navarro-Nilsson. Hold my calls, will you please?"

Maggie, a manicured-looking woman with a fashionably loose blonde bun, green pantsuit, and emerald stud earrings, nodded. "Of course, Mr. Keller."

"Umm, excuse me?" Julia walked through the door with a *Bennett J Keller* nameplate next to it.

"Yes?" Bennett pointed to a brown tufted leather chair against the wall.

"My name is Julia. Like Joo-lee-UH. Not Julie like Julie Andrews but Julie-UH like Julia Child, Julia Louis-Dreyfus, and Julia Roberts."

"Oh, please forgive me." Bennett sat in an identical chair on the other side of a small round coffee table. "I'm sorry I didn't pay closer attention to the 'uh.' "

"No worries. You're no different than most people who get it wrong. I mean, you *are* different. You're the publisher—and very tall and brawny. Do people say 'brawny' anymore?" She eyeballed his desk. Stacks of newspapers, colored folders, loose sticky notes, two open laptops, trade magazines, and Cascade City Coffee to-go cups covered every inch.

"I'm former newsroom," he said as if reading her mind.

"News dump is more like it." She rubbed her palms on her overstretched gray sweater with those annoying little pills that form on fabric from too much chafing. "Sheesh, please excuse me. I'm honest to a fault sometimes. Don't take offense."

"None taken. So, Joo-lee-UH, why don't you tell me about the call center? It's where many of our best people got their start and worked their way up. And I imagine it's one of the most informative places one can be—

where our employees speak directly to our readers every day of the year."

"I'm happy to tell you about the call center, Mr. Keller, but if I may, I'd like to speak to you about a different topic. One of even greater importance."

"Ohhh-kay. What topic is that?"

"The sale of the paper—or the potential sale of the paper. It's true—you want to sell? I've been wondering about the model at *The Fort Worth Free Press*. Have you considered that? I might know someone who can help."

Chapter Twenty-Two

January 27, 2017—continued

Paloma sat on a high-back bench facing the beach outside her bed and breakfast. She wore red slacks, a matching turtleneck, a silver Russian mink coat with a black stone marten collar, high-heeled black boots, a fluffy white hat, and her thirty-thousand-dollar platinum ring with a five-carat chocolate diamond center stone. She liked to make an impression.

Emerson Mathis pulled up in his silvery-blue sports car and stepped into the parking lot. Paloma looked him over. He had the shape and height of one of those blow-up clowns you punch but pop back up. The sun's rays ricocheted off his glossy balding head. Ana Mendoza was right when she said the man had no neck.

"Ms. Martin, I presume? I'm Emerson Mathis. It's a pleasure to meet you," he said with a slight bow and practiced politician's smile.

"Yes, hello, Senator Mathis. The pleasure is all mine," she said, using her *gringa* voice, hoping she could, at some point, finagle her way into a conversation about Booth's Hispanic household help.

"Won't you have a seat?" She patted the spot next to her on the bench.

"Thank you. Isaiah O'Conner, the Board President

at St. Luke's Parish, requested that I meet with you. Of course, I said 'yes.' Anyone interested in furthering St. Luke's mission is a friend of mine. I understand you're visiting little Cascade City from big ole Dallas. May I ask what brings you here?"

Paloma rehearsed the story with Julia beforehand—her fabricated background and beliefs and why she, a woman from out of state, would have a passion for donating to the Catholic church school fund in inconsequential Cascade City.

"My husband Stanley and I came to Cascade City often," she began. "He had countless business trips to Washington State as a venture capitalist. Your state is known for its creative genius, and the start-ups here have not disappointed. The Beachcomber Bed and Breakfast was our favorite place to stay. The natural beauty in this seaside town is spectacular; I'm sure you'll agree."

"It's why I retired here—that and the endless supply of fresh seafood. The misty fall and winter in Washington are a small price to pay for the beauty that surrounds us."

"We would have moved here in due time, but I'm afraid Stanley died from an aneurism in his forties, leaving me to raise two school-age children on my own. I retained our home in Dallas, mostly for them, but I still love this place. It's full of bittersweet memories."

Mathis made prayer hands and bowed his head. "I'm sorry for your loss. I am a widower myself. I lost my Angelica many years ago. Regarding Cascade City, I couldn't agree more with your assessment. What's *not* to like here?"

"Well, I'm not too fond of your politics. Or, more accurately, the politics of this state. I come from a place where we like rare steaks and our hands bloody from hunting and fishing or—shooting the occasional bad guy." She snickered. "We're an open-carry state—even in schools and grocery stores. The crazies are everywhere nowadays."

Mathis nodded vigorously. "Oh, I like you already, Ms. Martin."

"The northwest's practically a role model in unpatriotic behavior and Godlessness," Paloma continued. "The majority of Texans, especially away from the big cities, take traditional positions on issues such as school prayer, abstinence, Christian patriotism, and Sundays as holy days—to name a few. And don't even get me started on books with S-E-X talk in them. And offering classes in English *and* Spanish? Why don't those Mexicans learn to speak the language? I'm afraid the wall isn't working."

"I hail from Florida, as you know, and I've been fighting for Christian values my entire life," Mathis continued. "I even started a Perot for President Club in college. As a US Senator, I sponsored legislation promoting Christian education that trains students to understand the truth in the Bible. Learning to defend their faith and effectively share the Gospel allows young people to change the world through Christ. I consider it my crowning achievement."

"Did the legislation pass?" Paloma asked, already knowing the answer. Julia printed a stack of articles on the man and gave them to Paloma to read beforehand.

Mathis' face turned red as a Maraschino cherry. "No, but I still consider it an accomplishment. We nearly got the votes we needed, and it raised awareness."

"I admire that very much, Senator." Paloma turned

further inward so the tips of her knees touched his. "This is central to my interest in St. Luke's School Fund. Stanley and I discussed it before he passed into the Lord's loving arms. We wanted to leave a mark here in Cascade City."

"We'd be grateful, Carol. Is it okay if I call you 'Carol?' "

"Certainly, Emerson. May I call you Emerson?" Paloma flashed a bright smile.

Emerson moved his face to within a foot of hers. "You may call me anything you want," he said, winking. "Now, regarding the reason for our meeting today—I hope you don't find the question too obtuse. Do you have a donation amount in mind?"

Mathis' breath smelled of cigar and gum disease.

Paloma leaned back casually and sucked in her cheeks.

"I don't mean to rush you, but I'm sure you understand," he continued. "We're in a mad dash to raise enough funds to break ground on the new school by the fall, and your gift could make all the difference."

"I assure you it would be substantial—enough to meet or exceed your building fund goal and add an adjacent theatre space. We should discuss it further." Paloma looked at her watch. "I'm afraid you'll have to excuse me. I have a doctor's appointment I must get to."

"I see. I *do* hope you are well."

The wake from a nearby ferry boat crashed on the shore. Seagulls squawked and circled overhead as they eyeballed the sand for hermit crabs, clams, and sea stars that might have washed up.

"No, sadly, I am not." Paloma rested her dainty hand on Emerson Mathis' knee. "I don't have much time left.

Stage four triple-negative breast cancer." She pulled off her white fluffy hat and ran her hand over her thinning black tresses.

"What a tragedy—such a fine woman as yourself, and you're so young."

"Emerson, St. Luke's is not the only organization I am considering for my donation, but your visit with me today secures its place at the top of my list. I feel a kinship with you, Emerson. We have much in common—widowhood and our Christian values. Perhaps we can meet tomorrow night. I don't have much appetite these days, but I *have* been craving Mexican food." She shook her head and laughed. "If nothing else, the illegals are good in the kitchen."

"I know just the place. Mama Mendoza's isn't far away, and I'm a regular there. A friend of mine and I ate the lunch special there today. Perhaps you know of my friend—Percy Booth?"

"Percy Booth? Isn't he the inventor of that newfangled pillow I've seen on TV?"

"No." Mathis waved his hand. "He's a Hollywood star. Made some of the greatest movies of the1960s, mostly Westerns. Known all over the world, he is."

"I'm sorry, I don't know your friend. I'll be sure to look him up when I have time. Why don't you pick me up tomorrow at six o'clock?"

"Yes, of course. And Carol—about that doctor's appointment—I'll keep you in my thoughts and prayers."

****

Paloma walked gingerly past the front desk at the bed and breakfast, where a young woman stood folding cloth napkins.

"Stella, be a dear and bring me some port. And some decadent, fattening thing to go with. I'm done watching my waistline. If ever there was a time to indulge, this is it."

"Yes, Mrs. Navarro," Stella replied.

Paloma took one more step when her knees gave way, and she pitched forward and fell to the ground.

Stella rushed around her desk. "Are you all right, Mrs. Navarro?"

"I don't know, Stella. But be a dear and help me up."

****

Paloma settled in the wingback chair dressed in royalty-purple satin pajamas—each knee covered with a bag of ice wrapped in a paper towel. With a glass of Port and a plate of warm chocolate cookies on the bedside table, she picked up her cell and called Julia.

"Tomorrow—six p.m. Tell Ana Mendoza to make sure the recording gadget is on."

"I will," answered Julia. "How did it go with Mathis?"

"I've got him right where I want him."

****

Carmen and Kelvin sat on the sofa in his apartment, each with a TV tray and plateful of crispy chunks of potato scrambled with eggs, covered with melty cheese, and smothered in Louisiana hot sauce. Kelvin used the vinegary condiment on everything from macaroni salad to hamburgers.

"It's not much, but I was able to make it with ingredients you had in the refrigerator," she said. "It's cheap and easy. It's called '*papas con huevos.*' Someday I'll show you how if you want."

"I could've gotten us fast food or somethin'. You

don't have to cook for me, ya know."

"It's the least I can do. You've been so generous. You saved me, and that's not an exaggeration."

Kelvin picked up the TV clicker and turned off the game show he wasn't watching anyway. "I'm not doing anything more than anybody else woulda for someone in such a lot of trouble. I think you're a nice lady who's suffered more than a person should."

Carmen picked up her tray and set it aside. She folded her knees under her, softly pressed her lips against his, and let her tongue express what she wanted to say. A pins and needles sensation spread across her groin and shot up her back.

She'd never kissed a man before.

Kelvin pulled back. "Carmen, is this whatcha want?"

"What do you mean?" she asked, ready to kiss him again.

"Don't get me wrong; *I* want it, but you're in a terrible vulnerable state, and I promised myself I wouldn't take advantage. But—but—I gotta admit, you're the sweetest young lady I've ever met, and you're real pretty."

Carmen grabbed the hem of Kelvin's T-shirt and pulled it off. "Can I touch you?" She reached toward his sculpted abdominals.

"You surely may."

Her body warmed, and her cheeks flushed as she ran her fingertips over his rippled torso.

Kelvin's eyes softened as he took her T-shirt off. Grapefruit-size breasts nearly spilled over the top of her worn-out white bra—a hand-me-down Consuelo gave her in seventh grade. He cupped a breast with his left

174

hand and kissed her neck.

Someone knocked on the front door.

Kelvin sprang to an upright position.

Carmen pressed her back against the sofa and covered her mouth. "Who is it?" she murmured.

"Probably a delivery guy or somethin'. Bad timin', though." He walked over to the rocking chair and grabbed a patchwork quilt his Aunt Bernice made for him. "Wrap this around you. I'll shoo 'em away, whoever it is."

He bounded over to the front door and opened it a crack.

"Momma?"

"Surpriiiise!"

Carmen bolted into the bathroom but kept the door open enough to peek out.

"Oh, my God. Whatcha doin' here, Momma?"

"Don't take the Lord's name in vain, and don't keep me waitin' out here like some kine-a fool. Yer white neighbors gohn think some Black lady's tryin' ta break in."

"Sorry, Momma." Kelvin opened the door.

Carmen's hands and feet went cold. She closed her eyes and let out a long, quiet breath through her puckered mouth.

"Now, grab my suitcase, son. I know ya only got one room with a bed, so I figure you can sleep on the sofa."

Kelvin's mother hobbled to the rocking chair in herky-jerky movements. One of her black shoes had an elevated heel twice the height of its mate.

Kelvin grabbed his T-shirt off the couch, threw it over his head and glanced nervously at the two dirty plates on the TV trays.

"Get me somethin' ta drink, son, would ya? It's been a long day on that airplane, and they didn't give me nothin' but crackers an' water like I was some kinda prisoner-a-war. The first-class customers got a sandwich, some-a-them peanuts, an' a cocktail. What's this world comin' to? I paid good money for that flight." She smiled. "At least my short leg had enough room to stretch out."

Kelvin opened the refrigerator and peered at the carton of yogurt, a moldy tomato, orange juice, and leftover frozen dinner. "Why'd ya come all this way? You sure caught me by surprise."

"Your birthday's in two days. I thought we'd celebrate it toge…" His mom stopped mid-sentence. "Son?"

"Yes, Momma?"

"What is *that*?"

Kelvin froze. "What is what?"

Carmen followed the woman's gaze, and her stomach dropped like a bungee jumper from a crane.

"That." The woman pointed to the white bra lying on the floor. "Please, tell me that's not *yours*." She pushed herself to a stand and shuffled into Kelvin's room, presumably to look through his closet for man-size dresses and pumps.

Kelvin picked up the bra and handed it to Carmen through the bathroom door.

His mother watched him with narrowed eyes. "Whatcha got in there?"

"I don't see a way outta this, so I best just say it. There's a girl in my bathroom," Kelvin said. "Correction. A real nice young lady."

"Please tell me your kiddin'. Not *you*, my well-

176

mannered, God-fearin' son. Now, yer *brother*, I could understand, but you? No way."

Carmen stepped into the hall; her light brown skin flushed and splotchy. She introduced herself and apologized for dropping the bra on the floor—from a clean pile of laundry, she lied.

"Carmen Cooper, I'd like to introduce ya to my momma, R'Shawna De la Fosse. Momma—Carmen's a friend from work. She's livin' with me—but it ain't what ya think."

"Is that so? There's a girl hidin' in the bathroom an' a bra on the livin' room floor, but I'm all ears," R'Shawna said, giving Kelvin the side-eye.

"C'mon over here, Momma," he said. "I'll get you a cup of decaf, and then we'll fill you in."

Kelvin gave his mother a moment to sip her coffee before he and Carmen explained things. R'Shawna sat in rapt attention as they tag-teamed telling the story.

She scolded her son for not telling her sooner but took it surprisingly well. She even praised him for wanting to save Carmen and her mom from Booth, who starred in 1964's *Tale of One-Eyed Nate*, which, ironically enough, was a movie choice available to the passengers on the flight from Oklahoma to Seattle.

Chapter Twenty-Three

January 28, 2017
The Cascade City Chronicle

"Kimchee Manufacturing Plant Opens—Area Residents Cry Foul—Foul Odor That Is"

Julia packed the baby bag with all the necessities for a trip to the aquarium. Toting the stroller in one hand and Trey on one hip, Charlie headed down the stairs toward the unfinished basement and door to the garage.

The doorbell rang, and Julia hurried over. "Uhhh—hi." She tipped her head to the side. "What are you doing here? We're just on our way out."

"Don't be rude, Julia. Invite me in. It's cold as a witch's breast out here."

"You mean 'tit?' "

Paloma stomped her foot. "You do that just to upset me."

"We're headed to the aquarium with Trey. See? I've got my coat on. Charlie's already in the car with the baby."

Paloma eyeballed a side pouch on the baby bag. "Are those candies I see in there? They can't possibly be for my grandson."

"How do you know? Maybe he's the first infant ever

born with surprising chocolate-covered-almond-eating talents."

"*Aye, Mija.* What are you now? A size fourteen? I will not shop for you in the chunky department."

Julia dropped the baby bag and put a hand on her size-sixteen hip.

"Who says you need to shop for me at all? Don't buy me any clothes. Okay? Good. Because you know what? I don't like you buying me size-ten clothes when you know damn well I'm bigger than that. Then I have to tell you they don't fit and watch you pout. I'm done with it. And don't buy me any more size-eight shoes, either. My toes are gnarled enough as it is from a childhood of shoving my big feet into little shoes. Okay? My 'boat feet,' as you call them, are fine the way they are, thank you very much. Now that we're clear on that, is there something specific you came for because, as I said, we have plans for the day. Oh. And it's not called the 'chunky department'; it's the women's plus department. Calling it the 'chunky department' is an insult to all the curvy goddesses in the world, including me."

Paloma glanced at the sofa with the checkered past, pulled her chin and lips back, and gingerly lowered herself onto it. She blinked a few times, sniffled, swallowed, and cried—a few tears at first and then a torrent.

Never, ever had Julia seen her mother cry. She stood for a moment, stunned and unsure what to do. "I'm sorry, Mamá," she said. "That was rude of me. Do you want to come to the aquarium with us? I should have invited you in the first place. I'm sorry—I, I…"

"No, no…" Paloma pulled a handkerchief from her pink leather purse with the gold chain strap. "I don't like the smell of fish. I don't like fish—slimy things with googly eyes. I don't like animals. They stink to high heaven. Cows. Horses. All of them. I don't even like puppies," she sniveled and blew her nose. "Who on God's green earth doesn't like puppies? Me, I tell you. I'm going to Hell. Saint Peter doesn't let puppy-haters into the pearly gates, does he?"

Who is this woman, and what did she do with my mother?

"Julia!" Charlie called from the bottom of the stairs. "We're waiting for you."

"My mother's here!" she yelled and sat beside Paloma. She thought about putting her arm around her but couldn't bring herself to do it. She tried and regretted it the day before. Paloma pulled back and asked, "What are you doing?" followed by, "Stop that nonsense."

"Mamá, what's wrong? I've never seen you like this."

"I'll be fine, *Mija*." Paloma took out a clean tissue and handed Julia the snot-soaked handkerchief. "Wash that on a delicate—cycle—and lay it out—to dry." Her breath hitched in her throat. "I don't know what came over me. Just tired, I guess. I've had a lot on my mind—worries. Regrets. You and my grandson. I came today to make you a meal. Is there something wrong with that?"

"Of course not. That's very sweet of you." Julia wrinkled her nose and leaned in to examine the top of Paloma's head. "Whoa. I can see your scalp."

Paloma sat up straight and smoothed her wool pencil skirt.

"Mamá? Why are you losing your hair?" Julia asked, putting an arm around her stomach as if that would calm the butterflies inside.

"You've just never seen it short. The up-do covered up how thin it is. Why do you think I wore it like that for so long?"

Charlie appeared and set the car seat by Paloma's feet.

"Aye, Raulito," Paloma cooed. "Your *abuelita* loves you very much—so much that I've decided to leave Dallas for good. I don't want to miss another day, so I bought the three thousand square foot house around the block: four bedrooms, three baths, triple-car garage on a corner lot. I'll keep the Dallas house if you two want to move there someday. Or would you prefer that I sell it and buy you a small plane and an airfield? You have quite a successful airplane manufacturer just up the road from here—it's the land of planes," she snickered, "and plain Janes."

"Not funny, Mother," Julia said flatly.

"Suit yourself." Paloma peered into a pocket mirror she fished out of her purse and frowned. "I'm getting too many wrinkles. Lucky for me, I still have my girlish figure. Carlos, unbuckle this child, will you?"

Julia felt light-headed. *Shit, crap, doo-doo. Did she say she's moving here?*

Charlie unhooked Trey's car seat straps and handed him to Paloma.

Cheek to cheek with her grandson, Paloma found her smile again.

"I have a way with babies," she said.

****

Three hours later, with Trey taking his second nap, Paloma, Julia, and Charlie sat in the kitchen for a late lunch of tostadas with beans, cheese, and charred corn guacamole. After years of having a staff that cooked, cleaned, maintained the cars, drove her around, did the shopping, and generally kissed her itty bitty ass, Paloma could still command a kitchen.

Paloma dabbed her mouth with a napkin. "*Mija*, there are things in my past that I've never told you, and it's time you knew about the skeletons in my closet." She took a deep breath. "It's partly why I came to this Godforsaken corner of the country. You have marijuana shops *everywhere*, and the people here wear *functional* shoes—in broad daylight. Yiccchh. And *recycling*—give me a break." She rolled her eyes. "It's practically a religion. I threw a soda can in the garbage at Perry's downtown, and the doorman gave me the squinty eye like I was Charles Manson—or the Green River killer. Isn't he from around here? And Ted Bundy, too? Why so many serial killers? Hmmpf. The lack of sun must short-circuit the brain."

"Mamá, forget the Green River killer. You said you wanted to talk about your past."

"Yes, yes, okay. I've grappled with this for a long time. Should I tell you? Should I not? Ultimately, my history, even the ugly parts, is your history, too. *Mija*, I'm tired of holding on to things that rot on the inside."

"Mamá, you're making me nervous. What could be so bad that you traveled all this way to tell me in person? Are you a felon or something? Did you gamble the inheritance away?"

"No, worse. I grew up poor—much poorer than you know. I thought nothing of it at the time because I was very young and didn't know any different, and many families around me weren't much better off. I started selling gum to tourists when I was five and begged for money and food where the tourists crossed the Rio

Grande bridge on foot. Mamá sold her jewelry, and Papá butchered goats and chickens to sell. He repaired watches on the side. They did their best, but it was never enough. I invented all sorts of lies over the years to hide my shame. I am truly sorry, *Mijita*."

"Why is being poor such a shame, and why come clean now?"

"There's more to the story. Carlos, get me a beer, will you?"

"You? Want a *beer*?" Charlie asked.

"Yes. Is that so hard to believe?"

"Yes," Charlie said.

Julia and her mother moved to the family room. Paloma backed up to the rocking chair, grabbed the arms, and carefully lowered herself. Julia brought her a throw blanket for her lap.

"Okay, Mamá. What else is there to tell me?" Julia asked, sitting cross-legged on the sofa, covering her muffin top and the muffin top above it with a throw pillow.

"I told you my inheritance came from a long-lost uncle, eh?"

"Right. Your Tío Ricardo."

"There is no Tío Ricardo. It came from my birth father."

"What? You were adopted?"

Charlie set a tall glass of beer on a side table, threw Julia a sideways glance, and disappeared.

"Not exactly adopted. But my father wasn't my biological parent," Paloma answered. "At fifteen, my mother worked at a restaurant in Mexico City. An older man who frequented there wooed her into his bed with promises of marriage and money. Mother was young and naïve. And with his soft hands, expensive leather jacket, and smooth talk, she believed him.

"He was married and dismissed my mother after a few months. She never saw him again. Seven months later, she had me. She sent a letter telling him about the birth, but he never replied, and that was that."

Julia covered her mouth. "So what was his name, and what happened to him? And what does he have to do with the inheritance?" Her insides felt buzzy and scrambled.

"Armando Davila died in 2010. He and his wife never had children. His last will and testament named me as the sole benefactor of his estate—his only child and one he never met."

"Jesus Christ, Mamá. And you kept this to yourself all these years?" Julia pushed on the sides of her face until her lips formed a fish mouth.

"I am an illegitimate child—a bastard. And I was dirt poor, to boot. Of course, I kept it to myself. No one else must know. Do I have your word?"

Julia felt a layer of sweat emerging between her breasts and down her back. "Yes, yes, now go on with the story."

"Davila Oil is Mexico's fourth-largest oil producer," Paloma continued. "The inheritance amounted to three hundred and eighty-eight million dollars. Since then, I've become somewhat of a stock market expert, and the original amount has appreciated nicely."

Julia stood up and gulped. "Are you shitting me? You never told me how much it was."

"Why must you talk like a drunken sailor when you get excited?"

"Sorry, Mamá. But holy fuck. That's a lot of

money."

"Did she say three hundred and something-something *million* dollars?" Charlie asked from the master bedroom doorway.

"Eavesdropping, Carlos?" Paloma asked.

"Holy fuck," Charlie muttered.

"Carlos!" the women shouted.

****

Paloma left to gussy up for her dinner with Emerson Mathis at six o'clock. "Wish me luck," she said to Julia before pulling away from the curb.

Oh. My. God. What other secrets have you been keeping, Mamá?

Chapter Twenty-Four

January 28, 2017—continued

Carmen sat at the kitchen counter and leafed through R'Shawna's February issue of *Southern Belle Magazine*.

R'Shawna stuck one hand in a family-size bag of fried pork rinds and held Carmen's childhood diary with the other. A can of root beer with a straw sat on the TV tray next to her.

"I made it to your first tenth-grade entry," she said. "I been readin' the diary since last night, an' my heart's been heavy ever since." She popped a handful of pork rinds in her mouth. "There's a famous book by Maya Angelou about a caged bird that sings. Loneliness, no sense of belongin', cruelty ever'where she turned. Your life's been like that. I'm sorry for you, sweetie. It doesn't get much sadder."

Carmen chewed on her lower lip. She remembered the first entry from tenth grade well—she'd read it three times since her English professor showed the author's quote on the big screen. She liked the anger the diary brought out of her. It felt good—like letting out a scream she'd been holding in her whole life.

She walked toward R'Shawna and tipped her head toward the diary. "Do you mind?"

"A'course," R'Shawna replied. "It's yours, after

all."

Tenth Grade
October 30, 2013
Dear Monica,
It's hard to write with my left hand; that's why I haven't written to you, although I'm getting better at it. Mami thinks I should wear the splint for a few more weeks. She made it from a cereal box, bandages from an old sheet and safety pins. I wear long sleeves so most people don't notice it but if anyone asks I tell them I tripped over a suitcase at home, but yeah, you guessed it. Papa Percy hit my arm against the stair railing because I used a fancy writing pen from his desk. I guess it's expensive but who cares? He never uses it. I would have put it back and I needed it for homework. I think it's broken (my wrist not the pen) but Mami set it straight before she wrapped it. You remember when he broke my cheek? I never got an X-ray but it felt like something broke in there. Hit me with a candlestick and the whole right side of my face swole up. That time he got mad because he found me in Dorthea's room smelling her old perfume that stunk nasty anyway. It's probably from the 1800s. Hah. He locks me in that room every time he gets mad. Like I haven't snooped out everything already. What else am I supposed to do when he locks me in there without books or food or TV or anything else to do?

Carmen put the diary down and bit her lower lip. R'Shawna motioned for her to come closer. "Come here, darlin'," she said. "This sofa's big enough for both our behinds."

R'Shawna squeezed Carmen like a toothpaste tube with a smidge of paste left inside. Her body felt squishy as a marshmallow and smelled like soap and talcum powder—not like her own ninety-pound mother who smelled of cleaning solution or whatever food she had on her apron.

"I can't believe what you been through!" R'Shawna said. "I never heard a such things. No wonder my Kelvin wants to help ya. An' about that dead wife a his. She's not still in that room, is she? The way you write it, I can't quite tell. Jus' thinkin' about it gives me the heebie-jeebies. I wouldn't put it past him. That Percy's nutty as a fruitcake. But I'm not tellin' you anythin' ya dohn already know."

"Dorthea's buried in the backyard under some rose bushes." Carmen scooted backward an inch and crisscrossed her legs atop the sofa cushion. "He made Mami help him do it."

R'Shawna clasped her hands. "Oh, my heavens. His poor wife never had a proper burial. She gotta be walkin' between earth an' heaven, lookin' for a place ta rest her troubled soul. Except for going to Hell, there ain't no worse fate."

"Dorthea died before I was born, but Papa Percy talks to her as if she's sitting there hanging on to his every word."

"Why you think he's so mean? This Papa Percy. What happened ta make him so terrible? He was a big Hollywood movie star with all the fame an' money a person could want. What he's doin' now is downright sinful."

"Not just sinful. It's *illegal*. I don't know what's made him so mean and crazy. But he's gotten drunker over time and more *loco en la cabeza*." She pointed at her temple and twirled her finger in little circles. "Always thinking someone's out to get him—his old

Hollywood studio, friends, fans, you name it. He's convinced people are cheating him, trying to steal from him or get him into trouble. Sometimes I feel sorry for him, 'cause I'm not sure how much he can help it."

"Well, he *should* be in trouble. I'll pray for the man, but he dohn have the right ta treat people like dirty dogs. Aren't you worried that he might be hurtin' your momma this very minute?"

Carmen shook her head. "He slaps her and stuff, but there's a screwed-up relationship there. She listens to him, and I don't know why. She acts like he's the hero who rescued her from the train tracks, not the man who trapped her and her daughter and beat them both." Carmen wiped away a tear. "He's going to pay for what he's done, and I'm going to get Mami out of there because she doesn't know better. Being cooped up and always afraid—it's like she's lost touch with reality."

"A'course. I understand, darlin'. But don't let spite poison your soul. Love heals better than spite ever will."

"The Bible speaks of jealousy, revenge, and hate. They're part of life, too."

"Revenge may be in the Bible, but that dohn make it right. You got a heart of gold, Carmen. Don't lose that sweetness. Do what ya gotta do an' then let it go."

"Yes, ma'am." Carmen licked her lips and swallowed to moisten her dry mouth. "I will do what I gotta do."

R'Shawna wrapped both arms around Carmen, pulled her into her bosom, and hugged her tight. The apartment door opened, and Kelvin walked in with a grocery bag.

"Hello, son. I almost finished readin' this little one's diary, an' I'm in shock. We've gotta do somethin' to help her an' her momma. That man's dangerous. I only saw one a his movies a long time ago, and juss because he's famous don't give him the right ta do what he's done ta this little one an' her momma. He was a handsome devil, though—I do admit that."

"Hang on there, Momma," Kelvin said, setting the bag on the kitchen counter. "There's a plan to get Consuelo out of there. Carmen's gonna tell her about it tonight."

"And this boss a yours at the paper's gonna write a story 'bout everything when Consuelo's free of that monster?"

"Her friend Jerry from the newsroom's gonna do it," Kelvin replied, setting the groceries on the kitchen counter. "Julia's settin' a trap so they can use Percy's own words against him. She's pushin' the limits of the law with how she's going about it, but I hope it works."

R'Shawna glanced at Carmen. "You look like ya could use some ole fashioned southern cookin'. I'm gonna make ya fish—battered an' fried ta golden perfection. An' we'll have squash casserole with cheese, onions an' breadcrumbs, too. It'll knock your socks off. You'll need your strength for the big mission later tonight. Kelvin, you cannot let her go unaccompanied."

"Absolutely. This time I'm gonna go with her," Kelvin said.

"You are?" Carmen beamed.

Chapter Twenty-Five

January 29, 2017
The Cascade City Chronicle

"Love for the LoveLine Channel's Cast and Crew as Retail Sales Boom"

Carmen checked her watch. Two twelve a.m. Kelvin parked a block from Booth's house at six-six-eight-eight Overlook Drive. The season's first snow drifted and twirled through the early morning sky, twinkling under the street lamps. The row of mailboxes by the driveway stood like sentinels. Kelvin grabbed her small cold hand in his large toasty one. The smell of salty ocean air filled her nose. The train hugging the shoreline chug-chugged along until the sound faded.

"I used to hear that train and make up stories about the people on it—where they were going and the adventures they would have," Carmen said softly. "I felt helpless back then, sure that I'd be trapped in this house of horrors forever."

"I'm here for you now," Kelvin replied. "And you've never been helpless. You just had to figure out how to turn your pain into power."

They hugged and continued their ascent up the driveway until they reached Consuelo's window. Carmen used the tip of her finger to tap, tap, tap.

No response.

She tried again, louder.

The window slid open.

"Carmen?"

"Si, Mami."

"Carmen, *mi corazón. Dios mío*. The worry has been killing me. I beg of you. Come home."

"Are you crazy, Mami?" Carmen replied in Spanish. "He put a gun to my head. I'm getting you out of here." She squeezed her fists tight. "This place isn't a home—it's a prison."

"I can't leave. He won't sell me to the narcos if I stay quiet. He'll protect me, *Mija*. He'll protect you, too, but you *must* come home."

"Listen to me!" Carmen snapped. Her whole body trembled with frustration. "Tomorrow—the police will come…"

"I'm as good as dead if they do. They'll deport me. The people at the government office won't care if the narcos want me dead."

"The police will ask him about the stolen gun."

"What stolen gun?"

"The one he took from the movie set—the gun with the buffalos carved on the gold handle. It's worth a lot of money, and he stole it."

"I don't care about the gun."

"Mami, that's not the point. You run out the back door when they ask him about the gun. The police will come inside to look for you if you don't. Did you hear me? The police will find you if you don't leave. A friend will be waiting for you in the alley. He drives a…"

"I will not go."

In the moon's light, Carmen could see the glisten of

tears on her mother's cheeks.

"Mami, you're not thinking straight. He's got some kind of spell on you. I've gotten *help* for us. A big story will come out in the newspaper about how Papa Percy brought you here and forced you to…"

"You're not hearing me. I don't *want* to go. This is the only place I've known for nineteen years, and—and Mr. Booth is—he is…"

"What? He is *what*?"

An owl hooted in the distance. Carmen's face and neck felt hot and clammy despite the thirty-something-degree weather.

"I cannot say," Consuelo said.

"You can't say, or you won't say? What are you hiding from me? Why stay here when you have a chance to escape?"

"Percy Booth is your real father."

An electrical current zinged up Carmen's spine. Her mouth hung open in disbelief. "That's a lie, Mami," she hissed. "Why are you lying to me?" Her knees gave way before her mother could answer, and she crumpled.

Kelvin lunged forward. "What's goin' on?" he asked. "Oh, sweet Jesus. Let me help you," he said as he lifted Carmen to her feet and drew her in.

"Who are you talking to?" Booth roared as he opened Consuelo's bedroom door. "Carmen? You out there?"

Carmen felt it coming. The world spun as if she were being sucked into a vortex. The buzzing of a thousand bees filled her head, and then—nothing.

****

Julia woke up in bed alone and with a familiar feeling—like she'd gone ten rounds with a world

193

champion heavyweight boxer. Or smooshed by a thousand-pound anvil pushed off a ledge by Wile E. Coyote.

"Fuckity, fuck, fuck," she muttered as she dragged herself out of bed and into the bathroom, leaving the door open an inch to listen for Trey. "Ow, ow, ow." She sat on the toilet and lifted her sleep shirt. A pink streak about an inch long started at her left nipple and extended diagonally toward her navel. "Holy Hell. I've got shit to do today—very important shit."

"Are you talking to me?" Charlie called from the kitchen. "'cause I couldn't hear you."

"I thought you left to meet with your homework partners," Julia yelled back and winced. Even yelling hurt.

"What'd you say?" Charlie asked, poking his head into the bathroom.

Julia pointed. "Git. Don't come in here while I'm pooping." She frowned.

"Sorry, hon. I didn't know you were pooping. Gotta run—meeting Jon and Celeste at the the café on Maple Street to compile our research. I love their potato egg frittata thing—loads of bacon and cheese. I made you a cup of coffee. It's on the counter along with the Sunday paper. I'll only be gone a few hours. I'd kiss you goodbye, but errr—you know. You're pooping."

"We've already established that." She thought about telling him about the mastitis, but mid-shit was not the time. She'd wait until after dragging her sorry ass to Mama Mendoza's to pick up the flash drive with the voice recordings of Booth, Mathis, and her mamá.

They can't arrest me for recording them. Right? Hell's bells, I hope I'm right. Google said, "Recording someone without their consent is not illegal when one person has announced that the conversation is about to be recorded or transmitted." Does the tent card Alberto put on the table count as 'an announcement'? It better count, or I'll be locked in the slammer along with Booth. And so will Ana Mendoza.

****

Jerry spent weeks reading as much about Booth as possible, including fan sites and blogs. And then he hit the jackpot—a firsthand source—Buster Bishop, a seventy-five-year-old in Colorado who did Booth's stunt work back in the day.

Jerry sat on his slate gray-colored leather sofa in his condominium near Seattle's Volunteer Park, legs on a matching ottoman, freshly made cappuccino on the end table, and the newspaper spread out around him. Juan Carlos walked past, in his briefs, with a glass of freshly squeezed orange juice.

"I'll be in the office," Juan Carlos said. "I'll send emails to see if I can find an attorney for Consuelo and Carmen. Not sure if anyone does pro-bono work around here, and I don't mean Cascade City. I mean Puget Sound. You can't believe how many people come to us attorneys asking if we'll work for free. I may have to reach out to people in Portland and Boise to cast the net wide enough."

"If it's a big juicy story, they'll *love* the publicity. That should help you convince someone."

"I wish I could do it myself." Juan Carlos sipped his juice. "But I do real estate law. Tell me if Consuelo and Carmen need help suing a siding contractor or designating a historical landmark." He set his glass on the side table, stretched his arms above his head, and yawned. "I love what you're doing, honey. I love your passion for people and fighting for what's right."

"Oh yeah? Well, you're gorgeous, talented, intelligent, and utterly loveable. How'd I get so lucky?"

"Oh yeah? Well, you're an undercover investigative reporter now. Exciting. Plus, you can watch movies before the general public and eat out for a living. What's not hot about that? You're a superstar, baby. Now call that stuntman and break this story wide open. That's reporter talk, isn't it?"

"Uh-huh. And you go file a civil action or write a deposition. That's attorney talk, isn't it?" Jerry winked at Juan Carlos, grabbed his laptop, picked up his cell phone, and dialed. Buster answered on the second ring.

"Hello? Jerry?" came a craggy voice on the other end.

"Yes, sir." Jerry hit the speakerphone button. "This is Jeremiah Dean from *The Cascade City Chronicle*. Thanks again for agreeing to take my call."

"You bet," Buster said. "I never thought I'd get involved in something like this. I don't know what you're up to, but a reporter—coming out of the blue to ask me questions about my Hollywood days. Well, it must be important."

"It could be, yes. But before we get going, Buster, I need your agreement that what we discuss today is confidential. You'll be my 'Deep Throat' if you know what I mean."

"Deep Throat? Uh-oh. I don't like the sound of *that*. Is this some sex thing? What kind of story is this exactly?"

"No, sir. Deep Throat was the code name of the informant who fed information to Woodward and

Bernstein about the Watergate scandal. If it weren't for that confidential source, Nixon and his minions would never have been caught."

"Wait, is this about politics? I don't follow politics much—too depressing. I thought this had to do with my past as a stuntman."

"I'm looking for any information you can give me about Percy Booth. What he was like to work with, his family situation, personality, problems on the set. You knew him for what? Ten years?"

"More like forty. We stayed in touch off and on even after Percy left the profession. Started getting kinda funny in the head after a while, imagining people were out to get him and the like. He accused me of following him to Washington State if you can believe that. I live in Colorado, for Christ's sake, and why would I want to follow him? It rains up there half the year."

Jerry formed a fist and pulled his arm down mid-air in celebration. Forty years. Buster would have a treasure trove of information.

"Is Percy in some kind of trouble?" Buster asked.

"Do I have your word that you'll be my confidential informant? I will not reveal you as my source when and if I write a story unless you permit me, in writing, to use your name."

"Yes, you have my word," Buster answered. "Percy and I didn't exactly end our friendship on the best of terms, and I'd prefer to keep my name out of it. I think he's crazy as a loon, and his legion of fans can be worse."

"What else happened to the friendship besides him accusing you of following him to Washington?"

"You should have a little background about Percy before I get to that. Do you know much about his childhood?"

"No, I don't," Jerry admitted.

"Percy grew up with alcoholic parents—I mean real boozers. Beat the living daylights outta him. When his momma died, he got shipped to an orphanage in Fort Wayne, Indiana, then foster home after foster home. He didn't stay long in any of them. Percy skipped school and stole things from the corner store, even the foster parents' houses—money, jewelry, silver candy dishes he'd sell at the pawn shop. Never seemed to form attachments to no one. I think that's why he had all them wives. He couldn't settle down. He might a left 'em, so they wouldn't have a chance to do it first. He brought a young lady up from Mexico to take care of his last wife, Dorthea, and he didn't treat that lady too kindly. Joanne—I think that was her name. I'm not even sure what Percy did was legal. It's like he bought her or something—very shady deal. I never said nothin' to anyone else about it 'cause I didn't have proof, but I did tell Hilda, my wife at the time." Buster paused. "I'm sure she'd remember. I can't guarantee she'll talk to you though. I can give you her number if you want."

Jackpot.

****

Jerry left to pick up Stanford Simms, Booth's stepson, at the airport. Cascade City's uniformed finest would meet them at Booth's house at eight p.m., and at last, Consuelo would be free.

Chapter Twenty-Six

January 29, 2017— continued

With a body temperature of a hundred and three degrees, Julia sat in bed, sweating, aching, and fighting off the chills. Trey lay beside her, his chunky little toes in his mouth. She slipped the flash drive she got from Ana Mendoza into her laptop and grabbed her spiral-bound notebook and perfectly sharpened number two pencil off her nightstand.

She wrote "Recording Friday, January 27, 2017" at the top of the page and clicked on the first MP3 audio file. The conversation started with a perfunctory hello, how are you, what do you think of the weather, what's the lunch special, blah, blah, blah. Mathis and Booth kept their voices just above a whisper. Julia turned the volume up.

Mathis: What's happening with the daughter? You find her yet?

Booth: Shut up, you ass. Somebody might hear you.

Mathis: There's no one around us, Percy.

Booth: I don't trust the people who work here. Nosy sons a bitches.

Mathis: Calm down. What's going on with Carmen?

Booth: I caught her talking to Joanne outside the bedroom window, but she got away.

Mathis: You think she'll call the cops? Teenagers don't have the best judgment.

Booth: I hear noises in the house. What if the cops are setting up a sting operation? What if they already bugged my house?

Mathis: Sting operation? Jesus Christ. This isn't some detective show, Percy. I promise you—no one's recording your conversations.

Booth: Yes, yes, you're right. But I hear sounds—sounds I can't explain.

Mathis: I will not indulge your paranoid imaginings.

Booth: Fine. What's up with Magdalena? You hardly mention her. What is she? Forty?

Mathis: I don't know how old Lena is, and neither does she. (Mathis laughs.) She came from some backwoods town in Guatemala. By the time I got her, she had two kids, born on a dirt floor in some hut. (Mathis laughs.) That's how poor she was. Hell, I didn't kidnap her—I rescued her.

Booth: Ever give you any trouble?

Mathis: Nah. We have an understanding. She does what I say, and I mean everything, or she goes back to her shithole country with nothing but the clothes on her back. She's lucky to have me. Besides, I have her papers. (Laughs)

Booth: Do you see that guy over there? He looks like a cop. Or FBI.

Mathis: He looks like a guy who works at an insurance company or something.

Booth: He's looking at us.

Mathis: He's what—six tables away? Maybe he's a fan. You made lots of movies, remember? Sheesh. You have to stop this—you're sounding crazy as a loon, my friend.

Booth: Lower your voice. Where is that damn waiter? I need a drink, a strong one.

Mathis: Starting early today, Percy?

Booth: I sleep like shit. With Carmen gone and doing who knows what and Joanne crying for her, I can't get any peace. The drink calms my nerves.

Mathis: Admit it. Joanne drives you crazy, but part of you cares about her. How could you not? She's the mother of your child.

Booth: I don't want to talk about it.

Mathis: Hey, get this. Isaiah from St. Luke's called. Some woman from Dallas wants to donate to the school building fund, and I think she's loaded.

Booth: Why would a woman from Dallas want to donate to a church halfway across the country?

Mathis: I don't know, and I don't care. I'm doing God's work here, and He trumps all. Between me and Him, we'll get this Martin woman to open her checkbook.

Booth: We gotta go.

Mathis: What?

Booth: The guy at the table over there—are those headphones in his ears?

Julia played it three times and didn't write a single word in her notebook. Her pectoral muscles hurt too much to hold a writing utensil; plus, why ruin a perfectly sharpened pencil? The recording had the goods and then some. *Jerry's gonna flip out when he hears it.*

She wanted to call Jerry but had the energy of a dishrag. And her left breast had gone from having a small red streak to appearing like it could win a rindlesswatermelon lookalike contest. She'd call Jerry later and shock him with the news. Booth—guilty. Mathis—guilty. And was Booth not just Carmen's captor but her father? Was it consenual with Consuelo? Did Carmen know that Papa Percy was her actual papa? So many threads to untangle.

Trey dozed, and Julia tried to do the same, but myriad worries and miscellaneous thoughts roamed around her brain, bumping into each other. And, her body felt sticky and downright gelatinous.

A text came in on her work phone.

—Meet me tomorrow in my office at eight a.m. I have important news. Mei Tanaka.—

"I guess I'm not calling in sick tomorrow," Julia said to her two-and-a-half-month-old, who, in classic response, spit up sour milk on the clean, dryer-fresh bedsheets. She covered the blobby white chunks and the stink with a T-shirt Charlie left on the edge of the bed.

A minute later, her phone rang.

"Hello?"

"It's—your mother."

"Oh, it's you."

"What kind of—greeting is that?" Paloma replied.

"I thought you were Charlie. Did you climb a bunch of stairs? You sound out of breath."

"Stop the histrionics. I just woke up from a nap. And what a nap it was. I had a doozy of a dream."

"I'm waiting for Charlie to come home." Julia stuck a thermometer in her mouth.

"You can wait for Carlos and listen to my dream at the same time, can't you? It started with a cheetah in the jungle wearing a fabulous turquoise choker necklace, and it spoke to me—the cheetah, not the necklace."

Julia pulled the thermometer out so she could talk—already one hundred degrees, and she'd only held it there for fifteen seconds.

"Mamá, have you thought about what you want to do with the inheritance money? I have an idea I want to discuss with…"

"I'm not finished telling you my dream."

"Another time, Mamá, okay? I have something important to discuss with you."

"I bought you a turquoise necklace."

"Huh?"

"Like in the dream. It's a sign that you need a turquoise necklace. I know you're sort of *earthy*, so I figured you'd like it. Right? A Navajo woman in Santa Fe made it. Found it in a high-end magazine in the lobby of the Beachcomber. The young lady at the front desk ordered it for me."

"Thanks, Mamá. That was very thoughtful. Listen—the newspaper here is in a lot of trouble—like newspapers everywhere. *The Chronicle's* owners want to sell it to a hedge fund in Chicago. A lot of people could lose their jobs. We need a free press; it's included in the First Amendment to the Constitution. Did you know that? Thomas Jefferson said…"

"And why is this more important than my dream?"

"Julia? I'm home," Charlie called from the basement steps.

"Mamá, I've got to go."

"Did you listen to the recording of Mathis and me from last night?" Paloma asked.

"Not yet, but I did listen to the one with Booth and Mathis at their Friday lunch."

"He said something about a woman who lives with

him. I wasn't feeling well. Frankly, some of what he said went in one ear and out the other. The man's a real blabbermouth. Typical politician."

"I'll take a listen. Thanks, Mamá. And thanks again for the necklace." *I know she means well.*

"What about the free press and Thomas Jefferson? And what does my money have to do with it?"

"Oh, yeah. I was wondering if you'd be willing to give some of it to *The Cascade City Chronicle* to start an endowment fund. It could offset operating and administrative costs. Otherwise, the paper will get sold to a company that'll bleed it dry and then close it. A Fort Worth newspaper and others have done it successfully. But finding a donor is extremely hard, especially in a smaller town like Cascade City."

"If Thomas Jefferson thinks it's a good idea, it's fine by me. It'll be your money soon, anyway. If you want some of it now to save the measly little paper, what do I care? I wish you had as much interest in fine art and *Paris Fashion Week* as journalism, but you've always been strange. And speaking of Paris Fashion Week, my favorite French designer has a new line of purses and shoes coming out in the spring, and…"

"We'll talk again soon. Love you." Julia hung up. "Charlie?" she called. "I'm in the bedroom."

"Hi, sweetie. What are you doing in bed? It's four o'clock in the afternoon," he said.

"I feel like roadkill."

Charlie kissed Julia's forehead. "Holy hell, Julia. You feel like a furnace. Do you want me to get you a virtual visit with a doctor? Or drive you to a walk-in clinic?"

"I'd rather see Dr. Folger in the office. I'll leave

work early tomorrow. HR wants to talk to me about the Carlton thing in the morning."

"Oh geez. As if you need that headache with everything else you've got going on. You think they'll fire him?"

"I don't know. I'm sure Mei's interviewed him, and that's why he's avoiding me, although he *literally* ran into me on Thursday."

"What did he say?"

"I'm pretty sure he called me a bitch under his breath."

"What did you say?"

"I called him a bastard in a voice clear as a bell."

"Are you sure you don't want me to take you in to see a doctor *today*? What if it's serious? The walk-in clinic's open twenty-four seven."

"It's just a clogged milk duct. I've been through this before, remember?"

"Tell me if you change your mind." He kissed his fingertips and lay them against Julia's cheek. "Have you listened to the recording of your mother and Emerson Mathis?"

"No, but I got all I needed from the conversation between Mathis and Booth on Friday. This thing gets bigger and bigger every day. And tonight, the police show up at Booth's home so Consuelo can escape out the back door. My mother's paying for a room at The Lennox in Seattle. I don't think Booth will find her there. The reservation's under a different name."

"The Lennox costs five hundred bucks a night—for a cheap room."

"Mamá also paid for her to have a hot stone massage, a facial, and a manicure." Julia shook her head.

"Something's up with my mother, but I can't put my finger on it. She showed up at our door unannounced. She's leaving Dallas and her friends behind. She cut her hair, and I think she has pneumonia, but she won't admit it. Her cough sounds awful."

Chapter Twenty-Seven

January 29, 2017— late afternoon

Jerry and Stanford sat at The Ten, a swanky little bar between Tenth Avenue and Virginia Street in downtown Seattle. The techno-groove music pumped in synch with the beating of Jerry's heart. The story of a lifetime would make headlines with "By Jeremiah Dean" inked under it, hardcopy and online. He imagined himself being a hot commodity fielding offers from TV shows, publishing houses, and movie studios.

"Nigel, get me a vodka soda with lime. What would you like?" Jerry asked Stanford, a handsome man around fifty years old, bald with a close-cropped graying beard, green eyes, thick dark brows, a dimpled chin, and a classic Greek nose.

"Ginger Ale," Stanford said.

"A Ginger Ale for the man," Jerry told Nigel, the bartender. "You sure I can't get you something stronger?" he asked Stanford. "We're about to cross into territory neither of us has before. Could be a little freaky."

"I want all my wits about me when the cops show up at that bastard's door. I'll toast to our success afterward."

"When it's over, I'll take Consuelo to the Lennox

Hotel. We can have a drink in the bar there. Does that work?"

"Yeah, sure."

"You're an important player in this story. Depending on who gets involved, the local authorities will want to talk to you, and maybe the FBI. You committed to seeing this through?"

"I've been waiting for this for a long time. Percy made my life a living nightmare. I don't know why my mother put up with him."

"We've got about an hour before we drive to Booth's house." Jerry pulled out a reporter's notebook from his back pocket. "Okay if I ask you a few more questions?"

"Sure, anything that'll help nail Percy to the wall."

"Do you know if Consuelo was pregnant when she arrived from Mexico, or did she get pregnant afterward?"

"She was *not* pregnant when she arrived. That must have happened after my mother died, but based on Carmen's age, it couldn't have been too long after."

"Do you think Percy raped Consuelo?"

"I still think of her as 'Joanne.' That's what Percy and my mother called her. But back to your question—if Booth held Consuelo captive, why would she willingly have sex with him? It must have been rape."

"Have you heard of 'Stockholm Syndrome?' It's where captives start to identify with their captors, even sympathize with them and act on their behalf. I don't know if that's the case with Consuelo. I'll let investigators figure that out. Do you know why Booth brought Consuelo here, to begin with? He had lots of money—or I presume he did, being a movie star and everything. Why not *hire* someone to take care of

Dorthea, like normal people do?"

"I've wondered that myself, and frankly, I was never sure that Booth *didn't* hire Consuelo on the up and up. I suspected something crooked but couldn't confirm or deny it, and Consuelo wouldn't say. She spoke almost no English when she showed up. I presume Booth brought her over because it was cheaper to pay a *coyote* once and be done with it. Cheapest bastard ever. He wouldn't even turn on the heat in the winter. I slept in long johns under my sweatpants and a coat. And Consuelo was someone he could easily control. That's always been big with him—control."

"Did he show *you* any kindness?"

"When I was eleven, I blocked a cast-iron skillet to my head. I was trying to make scrambled eggs, and he said I was making too much noise. Does that answer your question?"

****

Carmen sat on the futon in the spare bedroom and called Julia on the flip phone she bought at the pawn shop. No answer.

"The police are going tonight to confront him about the stolen revolver," Carmen told Kelvin. "Jerry's going to wait behind the house for Mami to get in the car, but she said she won't leave Percy. When Mami doesn't come out, Jerry's going to wonder what happened. I called Julia and sent her a text, but she hasn't responded. What do I do? We need to let Jerry know."

Kelvin pulled Carmen to a stand and gave her a bear hug. "It'll all work out. You've done everything ya can."

Carmen rested against Kelvin's chest. "What would I do without you?"

****

When Kelvin stepped into the shower an hour later, she tucked the gun from the pawn shop in her waistband and left the apartment.

****

Paloma coughed up blood and phlegm and washed it down the sink. She placed her hands on her ribs. The bones stood out like rafters in an attic. "No more chemo," she told the Dallas and Seattle doctors. "I want to keep the remaining hairs on my head; gracias very much."

Her mind stirred with random memories, whether she wanted to face them or not: a delicious meal of beef stew and molasses bread at a little café in Arizona along Highway Six, her first kiss at age fifteen with Salvador Mendez in a record store, eating dog food a neighbor left on her back porch to fill her aching stomach, the moment she and Francisco learned they were expecting a girl. She wanted a boy. Francisco said he didn't care and that he'd be lovestruck either way.

She met Francisco at West Laredo High School at the start of their senior year. He spoke almost no English, having arrived from Monterrey a month before. A jolt of exhilaration shot through her when she saw him across the room in Geometry class. His wide shoulders, strong jawline, high cheekbones, and curly black hair reminded her of the actors she saw in the Mexican *telenovelas*. She moved quickly, offering Francisco English lessons after school. He was poor, and couldn't pay her, he said, but she didn't mind. They had that in common.

****

Carmen watched from an open spot in the thick bushes on the other side of Booth's massive driveway.

Two officers drove up with another man in the backseat of the cruiser. No lights. No siren. A tall man, bald with striking features and a close-shaven gray beard, got out of the car, bounded up the porch steps, and turned to the officers. He got a go-ahead signal and knocked on the front door.

Booth showed up in black silk pants and a burgundy dinner jacket. He stared at the man.

"Stanford? Good God. I hoped I'd seen the last of you," he said. "Why are you here?"

"I came to see these fine men put you in handcuffs, you son of a bitch," Stanford replied, moving aside, revealing the cop car behind him.

The officers approached.

Booth's eyes narrowed. "What is the meaning of this?"

"I'm Officer Alex Sherwood." A head taller than Booth, Sherwood made an imposing figure.

"This better be important. I don't like cops," Booth said.

"This is Officer Wally Watson," Sherwood replied. "We've come to inquire about an 1876 Colt single-action revolver used in Spectacle Studio's picture, *Bandido in the Badlands*."

"What about it?" snapped Booth. "I made that movie decades ago. How would I know where that stupid prop is?"

"Mr. Booth, may we come inside and speak to you about the revolver? You asked how we would know where that 'stupid prop' is, but I don't recall saying it was missing. I said we wanted to *ask* you about it."

Booth gritted his teeth. "No, you may not come inside my private property." He stepped outside, leaving the door open a crack. "Do you have a search warrant or what?"

Carmen aimed the gun at Booth's chest with shaky hands.

"Not yet, sir," Watkins answered. "We're working on that. We want to talk with you, sir, that's all." At five feet seven inches tall, with bushy gray hair, a stubby mustache, and a round belly, Watkins and Sherwood were a study in opposites.

Carmen cocked the gun.

"If you don't have a warrant, get off my property!" Booth shouted and slammed the door behind him.

Carmen dropped her arm and prayed the cops couldn't hear the thundering of her heart.

****

Jerry and Stanford reentered The Ten and found a blue suede booth against the wall near a fish tank the length of a yoga mat. He ordered a second Maker's Mark on the rocks. Stanford sipped a gin and tonic. Frank Sinatra's "Luck Be a Lady" played in the background.

"What do you think happened to Consuelo? She should have been there," Jerry said, squeezing his hands together. "Carmen needs to verify that Consuelo's okay." He used his little finger to swirl the ice around his whiskey glass. "I don't know what the recordings say that my friend Julia and her mother got, but I hope there's something we can use to nail him. Then the cops can arrest him for much more than a stolen gun."

Jerry's phone rang.

"Julia?"

"Jerry! Oh my God, did you go to Booth's? I just read a text from Carmen. Consuelo refused to leave."

"Oh, for fuck's sake, *that's* good news."

"How is that good news?"

"Stanford and I went to Booth's, and Consuelo

never came outside. We were sitting here at The Ten wondering if Percy did something to her, like knock her out—or worse. Do you have the recordings?"

"Jerry, we got him, and you won't believe what I heard."

Jerry's muscles tensed. "Tell me."

"Booth's not the only one with a domestic slave."

"Holy guacamole. You mean Mathis?" Jerry tipped his glass into his mouth and gulped the rest of his drink.

Chapter Twenty-Eight

January 30, 2017
The Cascade City Chronicle

"Keller Family in Talks with Chicago Company to Sell The Chronicle"
Julia grabbed the paper off her porch and tossed it in the front seat of the Cadillac. When she pulled into *The Chronicle's* parking lot with ten minutes to spare, she read the front page.

Local print news has been declining for years due to the loss of ad revenue and subscribers. The internet and social media platforms have contributed to the losses along with the evolution of cultural norms. Since 2005, the United States has lost more than 25% of its local publications at the rate of two a week. By 2025, academics predict the U.S. will lose one-third of its local papers, putting 70 million Americans, often in poor and rural areas, at risk of living in information voids.

In news deserts, as they've come to be known, government officials are no longer held responsible by the press for misdeeds. An uninformed population participates less in democratic processes such as voting and running for local office. Other repercussions include increased misinformation, heightened political divisions, and reduced public trust in media. However, surveys indicate that the public has more confidence in local press outlets than in national ones.

Although corporate and philanthropic funding in the recent past has contributed to numerous digital sites, these outlets tend to exist in technology-savvy urban areas with varied conventional and unconventional funding sources. Adopting a nonprofit model has resulted in some success for individual newsrooms.

Surviving newspapers have dramatically cut staff and lost readership. At the same time, conglomerates like Troy Media, Mathers Inc, Kim Enterprises, and Blye Global Corporation have bought vast shares of local papers throughout the country. These entities regularly sell or close unsuccessful newspapers within months of purchasing them and have no requirement to explain why.

Despite creative efforts, the Keller family, founders of The Cascade City Chronicle, has struggled to keep the presses running. Members, including the newly minted publisher, Bennett Keller, are talking with Troy Media about a potential sale. If it occurs, Troy vows to invest in the paper's infrastructure, boost newsroom resources, and contribute to a thriving local community with coverage that matters to Cascade City residents. Small and mid-size publishers nationwide doubt their intentions based on history with other newsprint organizations they've bought and closed.

A strong proponent of journalism with local roots, Mayor Jenny Leander has requested involvement in the matter.

****

Julia fell into a chair in Mei Tanaka's HR office. Her long hair hung loose and slightly frizzed. Perspiration trickled down her everywhere.

"You look awful, Julia," Mei began. "You better not be contagious because I can't get sick now. My son's about to have his tonsils out, and my partner's not up to the task. She'll faint at the sight of an IV needle or the first drop of blood. Even the hospital smell sends her over the edge."

"I have an infection. Inside my—mammary gland. I feel like total and complete crap, Mei."

"Phew. So not contagious. Have you seen a doctor? You look like you just crawled out of a cave."

Julia's mouth formed an upside-down horseshoe. "Thanks for being so—*truthful*. I'll see the doctor tomorrow or after work today."

"I'll try to make this quick before you can keel over on me. Look, Julia, I'm sorry to say this, especially with you feeling lousy, but Carlton's moving ahead with someone else for the call center senior manager position."

"Ummm—what?" Julia's head tipped back, and her eyes rolled up. "No, no, fuck nooo."

"I told him he should post the position because there are qualified people inside the company, and we, as a general rule, like to promote from within when we can."

"What'd he say?"

"That he planned to hire some guy named"—Mei looked at her laptop—"Richard Schmelzer from *The Seattle Sentinel*."

"That guy? He runs the call center there. I've met him before, and he's ancient." Mei wagged her finger in disapproval. "Yeah, I know," Julia continued. "Being old shouldn't disqualify him, but this Dick, I mean Richard, struggles to form complete sentences, Mei. He smells like moth balls, and his head must itch a lot because he scratches it constantly, and big chunks of something float around when he's doing it." Julia stuck her tongue out at the thought.

"Mr. Schmelzer told Carlton he wants to work at a smaller paper until he's ready to retire," Mei replied. "Less stress, I suppose."

"But he's like seventy years old. And why would we hire someone who's talking about retiring? That makes no sense. I've got lots of runway ahead of me. It's payback, and you know it. Carlton's punishing me for reporting him."

"I know this is tough to hear, Julia, but Carlton has lined up someone qualified to be his replacement."

Julia drooped in her chair. "What about the investigation?"

"I haven't found concrete evidence that Carlton sexually harassed you or said anything inappropriate about your ethnic background, although…"

"Although, what?"

"Some dude from our facilities crew stopped by this morning. He wants to talk with me about Carlton. The timing seems odd. Maybe he saw or heard something?"

"Facilities guy?"

"A Duncan McTavish—thick-rimmed black glasses, short dark hair. Janitorial staff. I made an appointment with him today at half past one."

"I wonder if he was the guy at Killian's the night Carlton and I were there. Some dude with black glasses watched the whole thing go down."

"I'll find out," Mei said.

Julia folded over at the middle. "I swear Carlton *has* harassed me. Repeatedly. He makes comments about my butt. About my bra size. He touches his ass with his finger and makes a *sssss*izzling sound when I walk by. Last week he asked what breast milk tastes like. He solicited sex from me at Killian's Billiard Club on January 20th, and I refused. And now I'm going to lose my job because I reported it. People don't come forward because of shit like this, Mei. It's why I waited so long to tell you."

"It's not that I don't believe you, Julia, but I can't *prove* your case. Whatever he did, he didn't do it within earshot of anyone else. I'll review it with my director to see if we can *make* Carlton post the job, but as it stands now, I can't punish him."

"I wanted to call in sick today, but I came in—for *this*. And it sucks. I am fucking furious." Fat tears fell onto her black maternity pantlegs.

"I'm sorry. I truly am. You want me to buy you a cup of coffee?"

"An iced coffee would be good, 'cause I'm fucking burning up, literally and figuratively. And yeah, I'll let you pay for it. I could be out of a job soon and begging on the streets." She pushed herself to a stand, took two unsteady steps, collapsed, and smacked her head full force at the base of the round bar of Mei's metal coat stand.

****

She opened her eyes and stared into the face of a man with curly black hair and enviable thick eyelashes. His name tag said, "Tompkins."

"Hot damn. Where am I?" Julia asked, her hair damp and plastered to her aching head.

"You're in an ambulance, ma'am," Tompkins replied. "We're almost at the hospital."

218

"Don't take me *there*." She tried to sit up. "*Hablas Español? Yo hablo Español.*"

The ambulance driver turned to look at Tompkins and laughed.

"I think you're a little confused, ma'am. That can happen with a high fever. But I do speak Spanish *un poco*." Tompkins held his thumb and forefinger an inch apart to demonstrate and then ran a thermometer thingamabob across her forehead. "Your fever is a hundred and five, which could be dangerous if it stays that way for long. The doctors will probably bring it down with cool compresses, IV fluids, and medication. But they'll need to determine the underlying cause. You hit your head pretty good, too. We've closed it with a couple of butterfly bandages, but you'll need stitches."

"Do you have ice cream in this truck? Does this truck play music?"

The guy in the driver's seat laughed again.

"Is this funny to you, pal?" she yelled.

"We'll let the ER docs decide what you can and can't eat or drink. That's kind of their call. Here we are—Cascade City Medical," Tompkins announced.

****

Julia opened her eyes, and Charlie slowly came into focus. "What's going on?"

"You're in the hospital, babe. The mastitis turned septic. They put you on antibiotics to clear it up. You've also got a nasty concussion from the fall. They stitched you up—eight stitches in all."

"Where's Trey?" She tried to push up on her elbows and flopped back down on the bed.

"I called Cassandra from daycare. I left the car seat for her, and she took him to our house after they closed.

She'll stay there as long as needed. I called your mother first, but she didn't answer." He bent over to kiss Julia on the forehead. "Your fever's coming down. They put an electric cooling blanket on you when you first arrived while they waited for the medication to kick in. Mei Tanaka called me on my cell and told me what had happened. I got here as fast as I could."

"Have you tried calling Mamá again? She can go to the house and relieve Cassandra."

"I've called her four times. Maybe her phone's turned off, or it ran out of charge. I can try The Beachcomber in a little bit."

"When can I get out of here? I was supposed to talk with Jerry this afternoon. As soon as he hears Booth and Mathis on the recording, we can call the police."

"I don't know when you can go home. Depending on how you respond to the antibiotics, you'll stay the night and possibly tomorrow. The doctor will check on you in the morning. And Jerry should be arriving any time." Charlie grabbed Julia's hand and kissed it.

"Charlie?"

"Hmmm?"

"Carlton's giving the call center position to Richard Schmelzer from *The Seattle Sentinel*. I gambled when I turned Carlton in and lost. It's retaliation—I'm sure of it." She tried straightening the sheets and blanket on the bed. "This thing looks like a band of Tasmanian devils has been living in it. Did I make this mess?"

Charlie sipped water from a paper cup, stood up, and fixed the bedding. "You haven't lost anything, babe. You've won. Turning that pervert in took a lot of guts. And I don't doubt that you and Jerry will see this through. You're brave, Julia. You're a class act. The firecracker I married is back. If you lose your job, we'll figure out our finances, even if we have to take out a loan from the Bank of Paloma."

"Oh Lord, I hope not."

Charlie exhaled loudly. "It's okay to need help occasionally, but I'm with you. We'll avoid asking your mother for money unless we have no choice. We'll talk about it more when you're home. I'm going to the cafeteria for a quick bite. You want anything?"

"No, thanks. I wouldn't feed the food here to my worst enemy. I remember it from the day after Trey was born. What do they have against salt, butter, sugar, chocolate, and everything bad for you anyway?"

"It's called a 'health' care organization for a reason, babe. Be right back."

Jerry came into the room as Charlie left.

"You didn't have to go through all this just to avoid seeing me," Jerry said as he tossed a paper bag on the hospital bed.

Julia opened it and pulled out a carton of 'Chocolate Cherry Seinfeld' ice cream. "It's shit like this that makes me love you, Jer. I hope you don't expect me to share."

"I brought *two* spoons."

Charlie rushed through the door, his eyebrows in the "up" position. "Your mother's here."

"Send her in," Julia replied.

"She's not here to see you. She's a patient on this floor."

Chapter Twenty-Nine

January 30, 2017— continued

Fat and fluffy snowflakes hung in the air before drifting to the ground and melting. Carmen stood at the front door of the Cascade City Municipal Court, looking out. R'Shawna teetered up the walkway, a cane in one hand and a white plastic bag in the other.

"Hello, darlin'. It's a big day for you. Here," R'Shawna said, holding out the bag. "I brought ya this. It was the best I could do under the circumstances."

"Thank you, ma'am," Carmen said. "I'm sure I'll love it."

They found their way into a poorly lit bathroom where Carmen could change out of her clothes and into the long white dress R'Shawna found at a secondhand store.

****

Jerry stood in the doorway of Julia's hospital room, the flash drive from Julia's purse in his hand. He promised to listen to the Booth-Mathis-Paloma conversations and call her later.

"I hope Paloma's okay," he told her. "I love you, honey girl. Take care of yourself. And enjoy the ice cream—solo. I can't believe I'm letting you have it all to yourself."

Julia pushed the red "call nurse" button clipped to the bed. The second shift nurse arrived within minutes.

"How can I help you, love?" he asked, his accent distinctly Carribean.

"Can I go see my mother?"

"Your mother?"

"Paloma Navarro. Why is she here?"

"Oh, that is your mother? I am not at liberty to share health information unless she give permission. She do not like the yellow hospital gown we put her in. No, no." He shook his finger. "She say it make her look sickly, which make me laugh because people who come to the hospital is sick. The laundry looks for *blue* gown, which your mother say would be all right, although she is not too pleased about that either. She tell me if she have to stay long, she will order something prettier from Palmer's Department Store."

"Will she have to stay here long?"

"I cannot say this to you."

"Oh, right. Damn confidentiality. Well, can I go to her room? I had no idea she was here."

"Of course, let me help you get out of bed. You must be careful. The infection seems to respond to the antibiotic, but you may still be weak and unsteady. Take it slow, my love."

Charlie looked on. "Do you want me to go with you, hon?"

"Uh-huh. I'll probably need moral support. Why in the world is Mamá here? She's had bladder infections in the past. That's probably it—she probably let one go on too long. Those can wreak havoc on a person's system. Or her cold got into her lungs. That cough of hers has been awful."

Julia pushed the IV pole toward room two-o-six, wearing green anti-slip hospital socks with sticky little pads on the bottom and two hospital gowns, one covering the front and the other covering the back.

"Thanks for the second gown," she told the nurse. "Nobody's going to see my hairy lower back today. It's a jungle back there."

****

Paloma lay still with closed eyes. Tubes ran to and from her nose, arm, and under the bedsheet. A catheter led to a urine bag hanging off the bed. A lima-bean-shaped plastic tub half-filled with bloody sputum sat on the table.

"What in the hell?" Julia squeaked. "Mamá? It's me. Can you hear me? What's wrong? Is it pneumonia?"

Charlie stared at the whiteboard on the wall.

Today is: Monday, January 30, 2017

Name: Paloma Martín Navarro

Room #: Two-o-six

Age: Forty-four

Allergies: none

Care Team: Dr. Shelley Lewis – Oncology, Nurse: Ajani Lawrence, Hospice Social Worker: Trina Albertsen, Minister: Paolo Shapiro

Activity Goals: N/A

Food Restrictions: clear liquids as tolerated

Julia walked into the private bathroom, sat on the toilet lid, grabbed some toilet paper, and blew her nose. "She has an oncologist?"

"Let's not get ahead of ourselves," Charlie said. "Maybe it's not as bad as it seems."

"It says 'Hospice' on the board, Charlie."

"Carlos?" Paloma mumbled. "Get me a diet soda. In

a glass. Plenty of ice."

Julia jumped off the toilet seat, IV pole and all. "Mamá. Why are you here?"

"Julia? Why are you hooked up to that thing? You look awful in that color. People with olive skin should never wear green or yellow. Ever. You could pass for an underripe banana in the best of times but more so in that gown."

"I have an infection, Mamá, but I'll be fine."

"Are those stitches in your head?"

Charlie pushed a chair next to Paloma's bed for Julia to sit.

"Never mind the stitches. What's wrong with you? The whiteboard says you're in hospice care."

"Oh. That. I have cancer. Would you or Carlos stop by The Beachcomber and get my makeup bag? I must look like something the Bigfoot dragged in, and I simply won't have it. I will not look like a worn-out old baglady, even in here."

"Mamá, forget about the makeup. What kind of cancer?"

"Breast, stage four." She sucked a few rumbly breaths in and out. "The first time was in 2012."

"The first time?"

"I didn't want to worry you. What would've been the point? It went into remission and came back. It happens, *Mija*. I *did* plan to tell you. It's why I came here in the first place."

Julia pressed her fingertips to the center of her forehead. "What the fuck?"

"*Aye, Mija*. I'd tell you to stop with the thug language, but what's the use? I can't change you. Please bring Raúlito when you can. I want to see my handsome grandson as much as I can before…" Paloma coughed foamy blood into the lima bean. "I never thought I would spit like a baseball player, yet here I am. Some of them even rearrange their private parts. On TV, no less. Tsk, tsk, tsk," she clicked her tongue. "Apparently, all the money in the world can't turn an overpaid lowbrow into a gentleman. What kind of mother raises her son to touch his privates for all the world to see?"

"Have the doctors said how long—how long…"

"To live? Not long, *Mija*. It's all over my body— lungs, bones, brain. There's nothing you or anyone else can do. I told them to stop the chemo."

Julia's heart thundered. "This can't be happening."

"I assure you it is. I've made mistakes in my past— plenty of them, and now I'm paying the price. I'm not a good person, *Mija*. Anything good in you came from your papá."

The buzz of a thousand tiny electrical currents bounced around inside Julia's head.

A woman from the housecleaning staff came and went.

Teardrops rolled off Julia's cheeks, splatting on the shiny waxed floor beneath her feet.

"Mamá?"

"Mmm?"

"A minute ago, you said you couldn't change me."

"Mmm."

"Why do you want to change me? Why have you *always* wanted to change me?" Julia rocked back and forth. Heel, toe, heel, toe. "I mean, what is so wrong with me?"

Paloma stared out the window. "How can it be forty and cloudy in Seattle and seventy with clear skies in

Dallas at the same time?" She fiddled with the edges of the thin hospital blanket. "Some things are hard to understand and harder to explain." She took a deep breath and coughed so hard it sounded like her innards might come out with it.

"Can I get you anything? You should put the oxygen mask back on," Julia said.

Paloma held her hand in the stop position. "Take my friend, Olga," she said, ignoring the oxygen mask suggestion. "Her great-grandmother drank like a fish, smoked like a chimney, and lived to the age of ninety-six. She had five husbands and sixteen children, none of whom she treated with a lick of kindness. Beat every one of them to within an inch of their lives. She went to bed one night and never woke up—the perfect death.

"And do you remember Miguel Vargas, our next-door neighbor in Laredo?"

Julia nodded. "He was my first older man crush—before Mr. Sanchez, my chemistry teacher."

"Miguel avoided fried foods, sweets, salt." Paloma held up a finger and bowed her head. "Give me a minute. My chest—hurts."

"We don't have to talk about this now."

The nurse poked his head into the room. Julia pointed to an imaginary wristwatch and held up five fingers. "Five minutes," she mouthed. The nurse nodded in understanding.

"We *do* have to talk about this now, Julia," Paloma said. "I'm running out of time."

Julia's temperature had returned to normal, but she felt clammy nonetheless. *Where is she going with this conversation, and what does it have to do with wanting to change me?*

"Now, where was I?" Paloma continued. "Oh, yes. Miguel ran marathons, went to church, volunteered at the food bank, didn't smoke, got early onset dementia, and died at forty-eight, leaving behind an adoring wife and two sons. By the end, he wore diapers and couldn't remember his children's names or how to tie his shoes. Why?"

Julia shrugged, unable to speak with tears running down her throat.

"The point is that sometimes there are no easy answers. I've never been one for introspection, *Mija*. It upsets me too much. But I'm sorry if I ever made you feel less-than. You've been a wonderful daughter, and you're so accomplished. You are your father's child. I was not there for you as a mother—I admit it. Children are messy and imperfect, and I wanted perfect. It was wrong of me."

Should I tell her how much hurt she's caused me? While there's still time? "It's okay, Mamá. You raised me right, and there was love behind everything you did. Despite our differences, I've always known that."

The nurse checked the numbers on the monitor.

"She said her chest hurts," Julia told him.

"De doctor approved morphine ta calm your breathing, Miss Navarro," he said in a volume somewhere between talking and shouting. "It'll help with the discomfort. I'll add it to your IV. I be right back, okay? I gotta get the medicine." He looked at Julia with a hint of pity on his face and left the room.

"*Dios mío*! I'm dying, not deaf," Paloma said with a frown. "Julia, I'm very tired. I'm going to close my eyes for a while. I shouldn't croak in the next few hours. I have much to tell you still. Will you turn off the light?"

She turned on her side, grabbed the plastic tub, and set it by her head.

****

Jerry plugged the flash drive into his laptop and played and replayed the audio recordings between Booth and Mathis at the restaurant on Friday and Paloma and Mathis at the same booth on Saturday. He could barely believe his ears—Julia and Paloma's plan to record conversations at Mamá Mendoza's restaurant won the day. Mathis and Booth admitted to trafficking women and holding them in deplorable conditions with threats of violence to keep them in place. Mathis alluded to raping the woman, Magdalena—and who knew if Booth had done the same to Consuelo? That would be a question for her at a later time.

And the following night at Mamá Mendoza's, Paloma asked Mathis if he lived alone.

"I have live-in help," he explained. "The Bible says, 'Wives, submit yourselves unto your own husbands, as it is fit in the Lord,' and you can't argue with the Lord. Lena resisted the idea after I brought her here, but she's come to enjoy the arrangement. As one who believes in God's word, I'm sure you understand."

"Lena is your wife, then?" Paloma asked after a coughing fit.

"No." Mathis chuckled. "She's the maid, but I treat her well, and she's thankful for the opportunities afforded her in the U.S."

"Where is she from?"

"Central America—one of those shithole countries."

"Does she want to go back?"

"Why would she? Now, let's talk about St. Luke's. What questions can I answer for you?"

"If I donate enough to fund a theatre on school grounds, would I have naming rights? I'd require that stipulation in writing."

"What name do you have in mind?"

"The Paloma Theatre."

"That's lovely, Carol. Why that name?"

"Because Paloma means dove, and doves symbolize peace."

Jerry stopped the recording. "Oh, Paloma. You are such a treasure," he said to himself. "The Paloma Theatre. That's a good one."

With the new explosive, nail-in-the-coffin information from the recordings, Jerry sent Julia a text: "It's time to get the police involved. We've got all we need to haul their asses to jail, and Juan Carlos has an attorney lined up for the women."

Julia texted back: "Can the police meet us at the hospital? I want to be part of the conversation, but I'm not leaving my mother."

****

January 31, 2017
The Cascade City Chronicle
"Shoving Matches Injure Two at Department Store Half-Off Undergarments Sale"

Julia and Jerry sat side by side on the neatly made bed in room three-twelve, an unused space the charge nurse on the third floor offered up for their meeting. With his laptop perched on the rolling metal bedside table, Jerry wrapped his arm around Julia for reassurance.

"I'm scared," Julia said. "We could have a happy ending here or…"

"Things could go down the shitter real quick." Jerry gave Julia's shoulder a little squeeze. "But they *won't*.

Okay? They *won't*. We're going to have to trust the police."

Assistant Chief Kermit Harrelson, a portly man with an uncanny resemblance to Santa Claus, and Sargeant Marcia Christiansen, a middle-aged woman with slicked-back bleached-blonde hair and a spray-on orange tan, entered the room and sat in chairs by a little round table near the window.

"What's this all about?" Harrelson asked. "It better be good because parking was a bitch, and Sargeant Christiansen and I have a lot of important work to do."

Julia glanced at her lined yellow notepad, where she'd carefully written a list of points she wanted to make. "We have proof that two prominent Cascade City residents, Percy Booth and Emerson Mathis, have engaged in human trafficking and domestic slavery for nineteen and twenty years, respectively. Captive women are in their homes as we speak. Is that enough to make that bitch of a parking situation worth your while?"

Sargeant Christiansen choked on her coffee. "You *what*?"

Harrelson stood up and put his fleshy hands on his hips. "Is this a joke?"

"We're serious as a heart attack," Jerry replied.

Julia reached over and touched Jerry's knee. "Or cancer."

Jerry leaned over and pecked her cheek. "I'm so sorry," he whispered.

"What kind of proof you got?" Sargeant Christiansen asked.

"Let me lay it all out for you," Julia said, consulting her neatly written notes.

Fifteen minutes later, Harrelson stood and hiked his

pants farther up his belly. "Get Chief Drake on the line. Pronto," he told Christiansen.

Chapter Thirty

January 31, 2017— continued

R'Shawna sat in the rocking chair in Kelvin's apartment with a small brown suitcase at her feet. Sunshine came through the blinds and spread across the room.

"Thanks for offering to stay at the hotel tonight," Carmen said. "You don't have to do that. Really. We'd love to have you here."

"I insist, darlin'," R'Shawna said. "It's your honeymoon. Lordy, Lordy, I can't believe I'm sayin' that. My Kelvin is a married man."

"You've been very understanding, Mrs. De la Fosse. I wouldn't have blamed you if you'd been upset. It all happened so fast."

"It's love, honey. God's hands are all over this. A'course, I can understand how someone would fall for my Kelvin. He's one in a million, ain't he?"

"Yes, ma'am."

"Call me 'R'Shawna.' We're related now." R'Shawna tapped her finger on her temple. "Darlin'? I been thinkin'. Consuelo's gonna need a place to live when all is said and done. I have an extra room in my house, an' I'm blessed ta have church friends that'll take her in like she's been one a us all along. Ya think

Consuelo'll come ta Oklahoma? I don't wanna grow old alone, an' your momma's gonna need someplace ta go. Maybe this whole situation'll be some kinda blessin' for us both. Korey, my other son, lives nearby, and between him and Kelvin, they'll keep you and yer momma safe."

"That's a sweet offer," Carmen said, still dressed in the white ruffly gown, a preteen girls' size medium, R'Shawna bought an hour before the courthouse wedding. "Let's get my mother out of that dungeon first and see where things go. Everything's so confusing right now. I gave her a chance to escape, and she refused. I can't understand it."

"It's gohn be okay—I just know it. Kelvin an' I'll be here with ya and yer momma for as long as ya need. An' who knows what's gohn happen to yer poppa. Jail, I guess?"

Carmen touched a throbbing vein on her forehead. "I will never accept that man as my father."

Kelvin came out of the bedroom, hopping around as he pulled on a tennis shoe. "Let's go, Momma. I'll drop ya off and pick ya up tomorrow when I'm off work."

Carmen waved goodbye.

When she looked out the window and saw Kelvin's car pull out of the parking garage, she pulled the handgun from the front pocket of a hooded sweatshirt, wrapped it in a handtowel, and buried it in her backpack. She wasn't sure when or if she'd use it, but she wanted it handy, just in case.

The doorbell rang. Startled, she tiptoed over and saw Jerry through the peephole.

"I wanted to tell you in person. I have good news," he told her. "My partner, Juan Carlos, found you and your mother an attorney in Seattle, and she's a good one.

The name's Greta Bayless. I'll send you her contact info in a text. Gotta run. Lots to do."

****

She waited for Kelvin dressed in one of his undershirts and nothing more. He walked through the door and enveloped her in his long, muscular arms. She lay her head against him.

"I hope you don't regret marrying me," she said.

"I'll never regret a thing when it comes to you." He ran his hands up and down her sides, exploring the indents of her waist. "We got a lot to solve, baby, but for tonight, let's try to forget our troubles. People might think we're crazy, but I swear I loved ya the moment our eyes met. I believe that *He*"—Kelvin pointed to the ceiling—"brought us together, and in time, everybody's gonna see we were right to do this. We're gonna get your momma out and grow old together, no matter what comes our way. Plus, nobody's gonna ship ya back to Mexico now. You're the wife of an American citizen, and that means you're…"

"An American," they said together.

****

Kelvin made love to her tenderly. It hurt the first time. She liked it more the second time. The foreplay was best the third time leading to an explosion of sensation as he pumped his hips into her from behind.

Hours later, she sat at the dinette table, thinking about her next move.

She grabbed her backpack, set it by the front door, and lay awake on the sofa most of the night.

****

Julia's infection cleared enough to get checked out of the hospital, but she refused to leave. Her mother may have been a pain in the ass her whole life, but she loved her. Charlie brought Trey for a short visit and went home around seven p.m. Julia napped in a chair designed for sitting, not sleeping. Her mother's breathing grew increasingly shallow. Her hands and feet felt cool to the touch.

"Mamá," Julia whispered. "We never had an easy relationship, did we? You wanted me to be someone I couldn't be, even when I tried. And I *did* try. I wanted to make you proud, but I was a thorn in your side—an embarrassment even. Why couldn't I make you happy? How come I was never enough?

"I've gotten bitter about it—please forgive me. I love you more than you know. I should have told you that more often. I said it lots of times as a kid, but you didn't say it back." She broke down crying. "You wouldn't say it back."

****

February 1, 2017
The Cascade City Chronicle
"Urban Sprawl—Cascade City Median House Price Tops Five Hundred Thousand"

The stubborn morning fog hovered as the sun rose over the Olympic mountains. The air smelled of the life below the Puget Sound waters—from dolphins and whales to tide pools teeming with clams and mussels, anemones, sea stars, and crabs.

Carmen entered Papa Percy's back door with her empty backpack slung over her shoulder. She entered the four-digit code into the alarm pad to turn it off, tiptoed up the stairs to Mami's room, closed the door softly, and bent over the bed.

"Mami," she murmured. "We've got to leave.

Quick. Before he wakes up."

Consuelo opened her eyes at half-mast. "Mija? Have you come home for good?"

"I'm going to take you away, Mami. We have a lawyer now. She's going to help us, and everything will be okay. I promise. Come on. Get dressed. I'll pack your things." She unzipped the backpack and headed for Consuelo's chest of drawers.

Consuelo swung her legs over the side of the bed and stood up in the same thin cotton night dress she brought with her in 1997. "I told you I won't go. He takes care of me. I am happy here. You must believe me," she pleaded.

Carmen pretended not to hear, pulled the double-action revolver out of a zippered pocket in the backpack, and held it up. "I've got this, just in case."

Consuelo looked at Carmen with wild, pleading eyes. "Put that away."

"I won't let him hurt us anymore," Carmen said, using her free hand to wipe the tears streaming down her cheeks.

The bedroom door swung open and smashed the wall behind it.

Consuelo screamed.

"What the hell is going on in here?" Booth snarled. His uncombed hair stood up in the back. His rumpled pajama top hung at an odd angle, the button-up front off by one.

Consuelo made the sign of the cross and dropped to her knees. "In the name of the Father, Son, and the Holy Ghost. Our Father, who art in heaven, hallowed be thy name…"

Booth pointed the gold-handled revolver at his

daughter. "I'll kill you, you little…"

Carmen lifted her handgun, a thirty-eight special, and aimed at his chest.

Booth bared his teeth, swung a long arm, and knocked it to the ground.

Consuelo got to her feet and launched herself toward Booth.

Booth teetered and tipped to the side, smashing into the wall beside the doorway.

Carmen swooped down to grab her handgun, then shoved an unsteady Booth into the hall. "You drunk dirtbag, you're never going to hurt us again," she screamed.

A shot went off.

The doorbell rang.

"Percy Booth? Open up. Police!"

The doorbell rang again—once—twice—three times, in rapid succession.

The front door burst open. Officers Sherwood and Watkins stood on the other side with guns drawn.

Booth lay at the base of the stairs, the banister above broken. His left leg bent outward at a right angle. A small pool of blood grew on the white marble floor. The stolen gold-handled gun with the buffalo engraving lay close by.

Sherwood rushed in and kneeled next to Booth. "Sir? Sir? Can you hear me?" No response. "Hold on for me. I'm going to get you some help." He pressed a button near his shoulder. "Unit twelve reporting. Request for medics to six-six-eight-eight Overlook Drive." He pushed two fingers against Booth's carotid artery, then put his ear to Booth's mouth. "Suspect down," he told the button. "Breathing shallow. Pulse one-twenty."

Watkins stepped in and looked around, his eyes settling on the bullet hole in the entryway wall adjacent to the Venetian chandelier.

Carmen and her mother stood at the top of the staircase, looking down. Carmen released the gun and watched it fall to the floor.

****

While Paloma slept, Julia sat in Paloma's room and read Jerry's draft article. Afterward, she wrote back.

Jer! The article sounds great, except that Carmen and Consuelo's points of view are not well-represented. You made it about Booth and Mathis. They're the big names that'll draw people in, but they're not the victims, the women who suffered for decades at the hands of those pricks.

You didn't include information about human trafficking and how people can get help. Silly man. Attached you will find my revisions. Don't be a turd and leave me off the byline. This story could be my swan song. I'm in talks with Bennett Keller. It's too early to know, but there's an operating model that could work for The Chronicle. I'd need to create an endowment fund with some of my mother's funds to cover the paper's operating expenses—with her permission. I'll explain more later. If it doesn't work out, bye-bye call center, adios to my job, and the death watch for The Chronicle begins.

XOXO,

Julia

PS: You made a few grammatical errors which I cheerfully corrected.

PS2: "hands of those pricks"(above) sounds funny, and what a visual. Can you imagine how small a prick's hands would be?

Julia sat in the fake leather reclining chair and looked at her mother. Under the sheet, her body might be mistaken for a girl's—five feet nothing and skinny as a broomstick. The heated air blowing from the air registers above didn't feel like heat—it felt cold. Julia rubbed the backs of her arms and then put her hands under her legs to warm them up.

Dr. Lewis, the oncologist, walked in, and Julia jumped to her feet. She told Julia that Paloma's blood pressure had dipped to eighty over fifty-five. Dangerously low. Her oxygen saturation was no better.

"She does not want lifesaving measures," Dr. Lewis said. "She signed a Do Not Resuscitate Order or 'DNR,' but I promise to keep her comfortable."

"When will she pass? How long?"

"It could be days. It could be tonight. I am sorry."

Julia thanked the doctor and held her mother's hand. Another hour went by before Paloma woke. Her skin looked yellowish-gray.

"*Mija*," Paloma said. "How long have you been there? You should be home with your son."

"I saw him earlier. He's with Charlie. I want to be with you."

"Very well, then. Listen to me. I wrote the instructions you'll need after I die: who to call, what to do, names, including the estate attorney and bank representative, phone numbers, and even my obituary. I did what I could to make it easier on you. It's all on a notepad at the bed and breakfast. Samantha at the front desk can get into the room safe where I put it. My attorney has the will. You're going to be a very rich woman, and my grandson will never want for a thing."

"He's still going to get a job when he turns sixteen," Julia quipped. "No freeloaders in our house. Have you seen the cell phone bills teenagers rack up?"

"Mija, I can't hold on much longer."

"Mamá, don't talk like that. You're not going to die anytime soon." Julia kissed her mother's soft, supple hand. "You *can't* die. I'm not ready for you to go. I need you. I have a son to raise, and I need you. I love you."

"I wish it were different, but this is my reality and yours. I have all the confidence in the world that you will be a wonderful mother, much better than I."

"Not true! That's not true. I'm afraid I'll be a terrible mother. It's hard, and sometimes it sucks. Why doesn't anyone talk about that? Is it just me? This feeling of failure? Will I ever stop feeling tired? And guilty that I'm not doing enough? How will I know if I'm doing it right? What if I screw him up?"

"Motherhood is hard for everyone. It's a struggle as much as it is a joy. Even when Trey is grown, you will still wonder if you are doing too much or too little or getting it *all* wrong. But he'll know that you did your best and love you regardless. All you can do is the best you can do."

"I like that, Mamá. All you can do is the best you can do."

Paloma pulled the plastic mask over her mouth. The *huuuhhhhhh* sound of the oxygen flowing in and out filled the room. The blood cuff monitor she wore started up. Paloma winced when it got to its tightest around her arm.

"We gave her morphine and lorazepam to ease her back and hip pain. Cancer in the bones affects those joints the most," the nurse said.

"Thank you," Julia said. She stared at the floor, vacillating between overwhelmed and numb. The exhaustion plagued her full-time. She pulled the handle on the chair and watched her legs swing out. Nabbing a light blanket at the foot of her mother's bed, she closed her eyes, dozed off, and dreamt of gargoyles with green glowing eyes. They hovered over her mother's bed.

Panicked, she yanked the IV pole off the floor and swung it with every ounce of force she could muster. The gargoyles hurtled across the room and smashed through the hospital window. She sighed in relief and then realized, in horror, that in the process, she had disconnected her mother from the machines keeping her alive.

Julia woke up with the blanket curled around her face, soaked in tears.

Chapter Thirty-One

February 2, 2017
The Cascade City Chronicle

"Retired Florida Senator Emerson Mathis and Movie Star Percy Booth Charged with Involuntary Domestic Servitude by Jeremiah Dean and Julia Navarro-Nilsson"

Cascade City, Washington
On Wednesday, February 1, 2017, two Cascade City police officers arrested Percy A. Booth, seventy-seven, and Emerson P. Mathis, sixty-eight, on charges of human trafficking and involuntary domestic servitude. Other charges may follow. Booth is recognized worldwide as the star in Bandido in the Badlands, Sheriff of Chaco Canyon, and Montana Wild, among others. Mathis is a retired Florida congressman known for his attempted legislation on Christian education in public school curriculum and proposed ban on a myriad of books in school libraries.

Booth fell from a two-story stairwell during an altercation with Consuelo and Carmen Camacho, the alleged victims in his household. He's currently being treated for serious but non-life-threatening injuries at Seattle's Harborview Medical Center and should make a full recovery. More information about his condition is being withheld due to privacy laws.

Mathis' alleged victim, Magdalena Ortega, and the Camachos are in an undisclosed location for their safety.

Booth's stepson, Stanford Simms of Los Angeles, and other firsthand sources corroborated the allegations associated with the charges. One damning piece of evidence, according to police, is an audio recording made on January 27, 2017, in which Percy Booth and Emerson Mathis spoke of their domestic servants—how they bought and brought them to the U.S. and used threats and physical harm to assert control. Ms. Ortega claims to have been sexually assaulted on more than one occasion, and Senator Mathis alludes to it in the recorded conversation. The defense attorneys will likely use the recordings' validity and lawfulness in this case.

Both men have denied any wrongdoing and refuse to answer questions under the direction of their attorneys.

Police investigators assert that Booth paid a human smuggler from Guadalajara, Mexico, to bring Consuelo Camacho, then nineteen, to Cascade City in 1997 under the guise of valid employment. Upon her arrival, Booth is believed to have confiscated Camacho's passport and identification and forced her to care for his fourth wife, Dorthea, who was dying of lymphoma.

After Dorthea's passing in January of 1998, Camacho stayed on without pay or medical care, with little food and no contact with the outside world. Less than a year later, Camacho gave birth to a daughter, Carmen, who was allowed to attend school but otherwise remained housebound, under threat of personal harm and deportation.

Carmen Camacho described a house of horrors when asked about her life with Booth. According to Ms. Camacho, serving a meal too hot or cold, peering out a window, or leaving a light on was punishable by starvation, beatings, and imprisonment in Dorthea's bedroom, locked from the outside.

Dorthea's corpse allegedly stayed in the room for months. Consuelo Camacho told her daughter that in the dark of night, she was forced to bury Dorthea Simms Booth in the backyard because Booth refused to part with the body. Authorities from the health district will supervise a dig starting tomorrow. An additional charge of improper disposal of a corpse could follow.

Booth purportedly threatened deportation to keep the women quiet and subservient to his every demand. Carmen recently escaped after an intoxicated Booth purportedly held a gun to her head. Newly married, Ms. Camacho quit college courses and her job to stay hidden from view and looks forward to a day when she can experience lasting freedom as an American citizen.

Dr. Sierra Wells, a UCLA researcher and practicing psychologist familiar with the case, believes the elder Camacho may suffer from "Stockholm syndrome," a condition in which captives develop a subconscious affinity and empathy toward their captor, which may, in part, account for why mother and daughter never attempted to escape. Carmen Camacho refers to her mother as a modern-day hero for keeping them alive during the nearly two-decade ordeal. "She's afraid for many reasons. There's been illegal behavior on both sides of the border, and I want all involved held accountable. My mother and I deserve safety and peace of mind."

The audio recordings reveal that, Mathis, a U.S. Senator (1988-1994), paid a trafficker to bring Magdalena Ortega from Guatemala in 1996, leaving her parents and two children behind. Authorities believe that Mathis may have convinced Booth to do the same two years later, as the men have been acquaintances since before that time.

Ms. Ortega, once a school teacher in her village, alleges that Mathis threatened to kill her if she dared to leave. She worked ten to twelve-hour days with no pay. Mathis kept food supplies locked. On occasion, Ms. Ortega resorted to eating bird food from the feeders in a neighbor's yard. Mathis, she said, often coerced her into sexual relations by offering food in exchange.

Greta Bayless of Seattle, an immigration attorney at Bayless, Moore, and Teal, represents Ms. Ortega, Consuelo, and Carmen Camacho. Juan Carlos Rivera of Mason Law will assist with the case.

"The Camachos and Ms. Ortega have endured significant loss and trauma at the hands of their captors. They deserve our support for their bravery and quiet perseverance in harrowing, brutal circumstances. They survived. By God, they survived," said Ms. Bayless.

Cascade City, Washington, commonly associated with its pristine beaches and quaint shop fronts, has enjoyed a low crime rate compared to Seattle, its larger neighbor to the south. Cascade City Mayor Jenny Leander was shocked to hear of the charge against Booth and Mathis, especially one "involving such callousness and cruelty." She vowed to assist Police Chief Kathleen Drake with the investigation in any way she could.

Involuntary domestic servitude is a type of human

trafficking in which a worker is not free to leave and is underpaid or made to work for free. Many do not receive the essential benefits and protections commonly extended to other workers. Women, in particular, confront abuse such as harassment and exploitation, including sexual and gender-based violence. Some general indicators of these unlawful situations include supposed employees who:

> *have no independent income*
> *cannot leave home unaccompanied*
> *do not have the same quality/quantity of food*
> *are prevented from contact with family and friends*
> *are not allowed to seek professional medical care*
> *suffer from exhaustion, weight loss, malnutrition,*

physical injuries

Booth and Mathis will appear in court on Friday, February 3rd. Booth will appear virtually due to his fall from the staircase, resulting in a compound leg fracture and head injury from which he is expected to recover.

If you suspect a case of human trafficking, call federal law enforcement to get help: U.S. Department of Homeland Security at 1-866-347-2423 twenty-four hours a day, seven days a week, every day of the year, or submit a tip online at www.ice.gov/tips.

This story is dedicated to the memory of Paloma Martín-Navarro.

****

July 2, 2017
The Cascade City Chronicle
"Mathis to Testify Against Booth by Jeremiah Dean and Julia Navarro-Nilsson"

Julia and Charlie sat side by side; the Sunday newspaper with the big headline and its freakishly awesome byline spread across the bed, their window and drapes open to let in the breeze. Star jasmine vines from the neighbor's yard grew over the top of the fence in a waterfall of sweet-smelling blooms—hydrangea bushes with purple flower bunches as big as dinner plates grew underneath. Charlie laid the comic section across Trey's lap. Trey banged on it, smiling each time it made a crash of crinkle sounds. At almost eight months, he could roll over in both directions, sit, pull to a stand, and hold conversations with his newfound vocabulary of "goo," "da-da-da," and "bah-bah-bah."

Charlie glanced at the sports section, and Julia concentrated on her knitting—light yellow baby booties.

Charlie set the paper down. "You want me to get you another cup of coffee?"

"Not right now. Thanks. Ummm, Charlie?"

"Hmmm?"

"Mei Tanaka left me a voicemail yesterday."

"The HR lady?"

"Yep. Now that the Kellers have a crap ton of money for the paper's operating expenses, they plan to buy a few smaller newspapers in Skagit Valley and the Spokane area. If they don't, those papers will fold." Julia leaned over and pulled Trey's shirt down over his little Buddha belly. He grabbed the plastic car keys rattle beside him and waved it around, smiling.

"And why did Mei call you?" Charlie asked.

"She wanted me to know that a bunch of positions are opening up, including one I might be interested in applying for."

"Does she know you're the one who created the endowment fund?"

"It was an anonymous donation. Only Bennett

Keller and Mamá's estate attorney knows—and Jerry."

"You've got Carlton's job now. I thought that's what you wanted."

"He quit before they could fire him, which sucks. He should have been ceremoniously kicked to the curb like the garbage that he is. Instead, he came in at night, grabbed his stuff, and slunk away like a weasel."

"Weasel's a good name for it. But what about doing his job?"

"It's not very challenging, and there's no career path. Did I mention that Jerry took the investigative reporter job at *The Seattle Sentinel*? He's milking the big story for all he can get, and good for him. It's his time to shine. That means *his* position will be open in the next week."

"You want to write restaurant and movie reviews?"

"I've got some writing cred now, remember? I'm Wonderella, the supersecret reporter no one expected." Julia kissed Charlie's cheek. "I could do the writing part from home. It'd be easier on me when baby number two comes." She held her knitting needles up to display a baby bootie.

Charlie's face flushed a lovely shade of tomato.

"What do you mean, 'baby number two'? As in, *someday*?"

"The moment a woman stops nursing, the egg machine inside her comes out of hibernation and starts dropping them puppies like clockwork."

"But you're still nursing."

"Only at night." Julia twirled her fingers through Trey's ringlets. "I thought that was enough to keep my egg machine from—from—laying eggs."

"So you're pregnant. You're telling me you're

pregnant?"

"We might want to start moving our stuff into that big house Mamá bought the next street over. Sooner rather than later. It's been sitting vacant all this time. Then we can sell this one or rent it."

"You're not kidding me?"

Julia shook her head.

"That's wonderful news," Charlie cried.

"If it's a girl, I want to name her Paloma."

Charlie came around the bed to hug her. "Holy crap. How are you feeling?"

"I find myself crying when I don't expect to. The littlest thing can set me off. Mamá's death happened so fast, and we left too many things unresolved. I may not have liked her much, but I loved her with all my heart. And about the pregnancy? I feel good, hon. All I can do is the best I can do, right? I will never be perfect, but I'm as perfect as I need to be, and that's enough." Julia dabbed her eyes with the corner of a throw blanket. "My mother taught me that."

****

September 5, 2017
Dear Monica,

Mami and I live in Willow, Oklahoma, with Kelvin and R'Shawna. I'm beyond happy we moved. Washington State has too many bad memories for us. Mami talks with a pastor at R'Shawna's church who did mission work in Jalisco, and I think it's helping her. We'll have to go to Seattle for the trial. Not sure when it'll start because I guess these things take forever.

Percy's on house arrest. He's not too much of a flight risk at his age, plus his health's deteriorated since the "accidental" fall from the stairs. I think I'll write a book when the trial's over. Who knows how many other victims are out there. Maybe they'll want to talk—if they can find someone they trust. They're the heroes of their own stories and they don't even know it.

A word about the author…

Nova García grew up in a distinctively Tex-Mex family with hot dogs and 4th of July fireworks, Sunday menudo and birthday piñatas, in equal measure. She spent much of her career in the newspaper business and lives in a picturesque Pacific Northwest town with her husband and three children. www.novagarcia.net

Thank you for purchasing
this publication of The Wild Rose Press, Inc.

For questions or more information
contact us at
info@thewildrosepress.com.

The Wild Rose Press, Inc.
www.thewildrosepress.com